Soul Chasers

The Decomposition Comedy

Rachel Armstrong
Available from NewCon Press

Songs for the Ecocene:

Origamy (2018)
Invisible Ecologies (2019)
Soul Chasers: The Decomposition Comedy (2020)

Soul Chasers

The Decomposition Comedy

Songs for the Ecocene III

Rachel Armstrong

NEWCON
PRESS

NewCon Press
England

First published in April 2020 by NewCon Press,
41 Wheatsheaf Road, Alconbury Weston, Cambs, PE28 4LF

NCP231 (limited edition hardback)
NCP232 (softback)

10 9 8 7 6 5 4 3 2 1

ISBN:

978-1-912950-56-0 (hardback)
978-1-912950-57-7 (softback)

Cover by Ian Whates

Text edited by Ian Whates
Book interior layout by Storm Constantine

For Rolf Hughes

"Although no organism can fully belong to both sets (life and death), organisms can be in many conditions (the very conditions that have created the debates about death) during which they do not fully belong to either... Death is a fuzzy set."

— Baruch Brody.

Journey

It's hammering down.

Puddles spill into sprawling rivers that spite the drains, flushing worms from their burrows along the grassy banks between pavement and road. With the Queen's Head pub in Sutton Valence melting into the rain in his rear-view mirror, William Mitchell grimaces as a passing car casts a curtain of water onto his windscreen, soiling it with drowned nature. Flicking his wipers onto full speed, he thinks about his evening spent celebrating an old school friend's joint engagement.

"Your turn next, mate!" says Ben Harper, his face splitting into a grin.

"Steady on, guys. I can't afford a place of my own yet," replies Will.

"But you're about to graduate as an aerospace engineer. You'll be a wealthy man," says Tom Singleton, the least single man in the universe, with a reputation of dating a minimum of two girls at any one time.

"Not until I've paid off my student load. Imperial College's fees have saddled me with debt for the best part of my career. I'm still living at home with my dad," says Will.

"Come on, surely there's *someone*," says Tom, knowingly. "What's that *ring* on your finger."

"This? My father gave it to me."

"Your dad? Be serious mate." Tom grabs Will's hand. "That's a *girl's* ring."

"What's that on top? It looks like a *pearl*," adds Ben. "Christ! It's ugly. Why do you wear it, anyway?"

"I get it. Thanks for your concern but, right now, getting hitched is not for me."

"You're missing out, genius," and Tom grins.

"Sure, I am," says Will, "but I'll manage just fine being on my own today."

While weather warnings have been at red alert, none predicted the current downpour. It's not just the rain smashing on the roof of the vehicle; the fields are also haemorrhaging so much water that clots of earth clog the drains, turning the roads into waterways.

"*Hazard ahead.*" The AI turns amber then red.

"Here we go," mutters Will, slipping into manual mode to take full control of the vehicle.

Along the Sutton Road he switches his headlights between full beam and dipped, steadily negotiating the swirling streams of water ahead.

Suddenly the car planes, spinning him around like a toy top.

The AI screams red, sending all kinds of instructions to the overdrive, but as Will has disabled the automatic controls it can't intervene. Removing his foot from the gas, he turns the lurching car towards the centre of the road.

A young woman wearing a loose white shirt steps out, staring right at him.

Stupid girl, what do you think you're doing?

Will slams on the brakes instinctively and the car churns the road like a washing machine.

"Oh god, no!" he says as he looks up from the dashboard. Somehow, the vehicle has come to a stop. He feels sick and his head hurts. His safety belt is tight. The streetlights seem grey. Did he lose consciousness?

Then he remembers the woman.

He didn't even see where she came from. Has he hit her?

Trembling, he gets out and wades towards the middle of the road, dreading he'll find a body. The car's blown a couple of circuits and is playing *Groningo*'s 'Happy Days'.

"*You're very stressed right now*," says the emotional mapping system. "*Breathe deeply, try to calm down. Or take a break.*"

Will holds his coat over his head ready to give it to the injured person, or horror, lay it over the deceased.

"Was she wearing white?" he asks the AI.

It emits an irritating whine.

"Just what I need, a demented bot," he says. "Can you replay the vision sensor? You should have been able to see her, even in this darkness."

The screen shows only noise.

"Perfectly useless," says Will.

He wades around the car using his feet to search for a soft body by touch and looks for signs of torn cloth – or anything. At what is usually a busy junction, a short distance from the Wheatsheaf pub, there is not another soul or car around. The sturdy walls of the nearby Maidstone cemetery and a line of sickly-looking trees seem to glare morosely at him.

"I wasn't travelling *that* fast," he mutters.

He walks a short distance down to the Pheasant Lane junction, wondering if the victim continued wandering in shock, but there is no sign of anyone. Deflated, he returns to the car where the water level is lapping at the door but has not yet leaked inside.

"Is it safe to drive on?" Will asks the AI.

"*Safety hazard due to severe weather. Temporary barriers are needed. No effective warning signs. Press once for OK. Validate. OK. OK. OK. OK. OK. OK. OK. OK. OK. OK. OK. OK. OK. OK. Press once for OK. Validate. OK. OK. OK. OK. OK. OK. OK. OK. OK. OK. OK. Press once for OK. Validate OK. OK. OK. OK. OK. OK. OK. OK. OK. OK. OK. OK. OK. OK.*"

"Oh, so *now*, you're talking."

Slamming the OK button, Will closes the door as rain smashes on the roof. Placing both hands firmly on the wheel, he breathes slowly and tries to think what to do. If he leaves the scene, he could be prosecuted for a hit and run. He can't have missed her. There has to be a body somewhere. He's going to have to report this incident.

"Christ, what a mess."

A river now runs where there used to be a junction and the windows are fogging up. He switches on the air conditioner to clear them and tries to ignore his sodden trouser cloth dragging on his legs and steady his nerves enough to drive to the police station.

Before pulling off, he checks his rear-view mirror and sees the drenched young woman in the back seat, next to all his books.

What took you so long?

"Oh, thank god! How long have you been here?"

"Hurry, we must get to Rochester Road, Aylesford."

"But… it's absolutely treacherous on the roads right now."

"It's terribly important. Please."

"See here, whoever-you-are. I'm not running a taxi service."

Immediately, he resents the comment as his uninvited passenger is obviously pregnant. He tries to read her face, but she's distracted, anxious, and won't look at him.

Will relents. Rochester Road is close to home and if she walks out in front of another car in her present condition, he'd never be able to forgive himself.

"Thank you! Please hurry," she says, as Will revs the engine to pull out.

"Let's get one thing straight," he says. "I'm doing the driving. You're the passenger and we're going nowhere fast in this weather."

"Rochester Road, Aylesford," the woman persists.

"Call me callous," says Will, "but this is as far as liberties go tonight, so you may as well sit back and enjoy the ride."

But the young woman can't relax. She sits forwards in the seat behind him, then rocks backwards hugging her knees, and he can't clearly see her in his rear-view mirror.

Where are we going?

Picking up an uninvited passenger makes Will feel uneasy but he is not as uncomfortable as he might be, if he could also see the two women beside her.

Book One
Winnie

Part I: Death

We the Dead

We thought the monsters beneath
Our beds were just imagined but
Each day, standing at the edge of
Existence, we were actually dying.
When our time came, we fell, totally
Unready, into pitiless nothingness.

Oh, horror! This is *not*nothingness.
Shapes swim about, *things* happen,
Creatures are at large. Fearful, we
Retreat into ourselves. Death is not
A distant possibility but shaping the
Murky present. Are we in purgatory?

In hindsight, our passing should have
Caused our belief in the afterworlds to
Disappear. It didn't. Death is not an
Ending but integral to life's symphony,
Where even the hardiest things decay;
Bones, capitals, continents and worlds.

Although some want to be kept alive
At all costs, we respect nature's course.
Untroubled by the same non-existence
We endured for aeons past before
We were born, our coming and going
Is inexorable. Death enriches us all.

Clone Identity

Grandmother slows right down as we pass the magnificent house in St. Andrew's Park on Barming Heath.

"Hurry up," I say. "I hate the drizzle, and we're late."

Twenty years of hell.

"Who are you talking to?"

She does this every time. It's so annoying.

"Not now, child," she says. "Such presence commands respect."

The one thing that would have made a difference, I think, would have been someone to talk to.

"We are sorry for your troubles."

When it was completed in 1833, the stern grey building with its many rows of windows, was known as the Kent County Lunatic Asylum, but it is mostly remembered as Oakwood Hospital. James Huxley, the brother of Thomas Henry Huxley, or "Darwin's Bulldog" on account of his vigorous defence of the theory of evolution, was superintendent here. Not only were they close, but the family also had a history of mental illness.

At its peak, the hospital housed over two thousand patients from London and the county of Kent. The capacity continued to grow after the Second World War, reaching a grand total of 2,000. Then, on November 1957, terror swept through the place when a fire broke out, resulting in the collapse of the ventilation tower, with tragic consequences for residents, staff and rescuers.

Although the asylum recovered from this harrowing event, government policy looked towards deinstitutionalisation: delivering mental health services in the community rather than through formal care. The patient population declined, and its services were transferred to Maidstone General Hospital. Soon afterwards, the abandoned building became the target for a series of arson attacks that resulted in the demolition of many of the buildings. Oakwood Hospital was finally converted into a residential estate, leaving St. Andrew's House and the surrounding area to the ambitions of property developers.

I would shut myself off. Maybe if depression had been explained to me earlier...

"I know you dream of living there. But we're close enough. Our

15

home on Tarragon Road is actually part of the site's development. Besides, it's the nearest we'll ever get to having anywhere grand."

I didn't have much faith in God when the kids died. When I wanted to die, he didn't want me, the old git. Now he's practically telling me he's got room for me. He can blooming well wait.

"Listen," says Grandmother.

I try not to. While many of the original buildings have gone, the vagrant souls that haunt the area have a habit of making themselves known to us.

I can't' stand that little bitch of a staff nurse. She demeans patients and loves it. She's always threatening us with transfer to a locked ward. She says we should be punished for nonconformity – like refusing to eat our meals. She's a nasty piece of work she is! Do you know what I've gone and done? I've left that slimy dinner for her just where I found it. Next time, I'll throw it at her.

"Come on," I say, "I'm getting wet. We'll be talking to the dead soon enough."

A staff nurse in a pale blue uniform swerves around the other side of a rippling puddle from us, stepping out into the road and pulls her overcoat tightly across her chest. She'd have crossed the road to avoid us if the traffic wasn't so heavy.

Who are these people?

Our close-shaven heads mark out our line of work as resurrection empaths, or *soul chasers*, if you prefer, so we are much more troubled by the attitudes of living than the dead.

The inner monologues of passers-by discuss us as we pass into the hospital atrium and I fold down my umbrella.

"They're simulacra – not real people."

"They're born without souls."

"Don't look at those baldies darling, they make bad things happen."

"If they catch your eye, they'll turn you crazy."

"I heard they actually eat the souls once they catch them."

"Mother of Jesus, be our protector and defender against all that is harmful or evil."

"Stay away from me!"

We continue along the faceless corridors with their whispering walls. It's hard to ignore the hostility.

"After more than eighty years of progress in cloning technology, you'd have thought that *singletons* would be used to us by now," I say.

"Prejudice doesn't die," replies Grandmother.

"I just don't understand it. The soul-bond that *identicals* of all filiations share – twins, triplets, quadruplets and so on – is neither visible nor measurable. So, why are we regarded as *other*?"

"We're not entirely invisible, child. Apart from looking very much alike, we also have a habit of standing out."

"Not *that* much," I say.

"Inventing our own private languages is hardly run-of-the-mill behaviour, child." "Nor is conversing with the dead. Historically, great attention has been paid to the slight variations between us, which are given unusual significance, most particularly since the advent of modern genetics. We have been routinely instrumentalised and regarded as 'living laboratories' in the service of science, for decoding the language of life."

"We're singled out for the strangest of prejudices, Grandmother," I say, as we reach the central staircase. "Besides, even if we *are* unconventional, we're hardly malevolent. That we share multiple life attractors with our siblings simply means that our vital force is strong and strengthens our sympathy for others."

"Strangely, they accuse *us* of not having souls, child," says Grandmother, "which some suppose are only acquired through the union of a *proper* 'father' and 'mother'. Since we have neither, by this reasoning, we are considered *less than human*."

We climb three flights of stairs into a passage way with branching corridors.

Pushing through a series of swing doors, we pass a group of medical students on placement at the Intensive Care Unit, who stare at us, then whisper when they believe we're out of earshot.

They're born with subtle birth defects, but you wouldn't know it.

Aren't they strange – a kind of medical apparatus.

Shocking to think there's a clear lack of a proper ethical framework for that business.

"Shouldn't we just tell people we can hear what they're thinking?" I ask. "Then, they might stand in our shoes for a moment, with compassion."

"That's a dreadful idea, child," says Grandmother. "Whatever fears people already harbour about us, would be made far worse by disclosing our *unnatural* qualities. Besides, our strong inner life-force can be put to good use here. Our sympathy with living things makes for *ideal* soul catchers – and all this chatter is making us late."

We swipe the door open and enter the changing rooms.

Counting the Not–Yet–Alive

The body architects have already begun their preparations as I step into the Intensive Care Unit.

"It's ridiculous that cloned tissues from the mortally injured, or deceased, have more social legitimacy than we do," I say.

"These procedures are generally only available on insurance premiums for the super-rich, child," says Grandmother. "*Resurrected* clones don't concede any status."

A technician transfers the gleaming metal flask that contains the primary culture harvested from the *technically deceased*, to a row of medical support staff who are organised around a rotating circular bench. Each adds, by hand, an ingredient of a prescribed cocktail of specific cell growth factors: nutrients, or hormones that accelerate the cell culture's development. Desirable strains are selected from the culture by cloning.

"There are an awful lot of samples to make sense of, Grandmother."

"It's a trauma case, child."

"There are more scientists than usual."

"They're making preparations for the SENSE international research study."

"Are we part of it, Grandmother?"

"Yes."

"What's it about?"

"It's establishing the technical limits of *death* within the field of resurrection medicine. I've read the proposal. It's impressive work."

"Is that my brief?" I grumble, but Grandmother's already disappeared into the empath suite.

It's strange just how fast she can move when the occasion takes her.

I linger awhile at the door of the reconstruction workshop, watching the body architects strike a fine balance between mimicking the structures of the original body and respecting the limits of growth in the donor cell system. All of these incredible processes take place under the surveillance of an AI and the whole process converges around a cocoon-like framework on which the various tissues and body parts come together as a whole.

"Get a move on, child," shouts Grandmother from the changing room.

Soul Chasers

"It's worse than I thought," says Grandmother. "This one is a mess."

Soul-catchers work together, like a pair of acrobats. Grandmother is the base, providing stability and equilibrium using the resurrection-support machines, while I, the flyer, surrender all sense and protective reflexes to deftly move through the decomposition landscape in search of the *right soul.* Coming face-to-face with all this technology gets my adrenaline racing. As much as I complain about the bureaucracy, I love this stuff.

"I'm up for a challenge," I say, peering over her shoulder but she raises her arm to stop me from scanning the notes of the deceased.

"Frankly, I'm concerned you're not experienced enough for this one, child," she says. "You've only ever worked on clean corpses, heart attacks, stroke and the occasional cancer, not something *this* complicated. Tests are showing these donor samples are contaminated by ancient, local soils, strange materials, unwanted particles and goodness knows what else."

"I'm ready for another level of complexity, Grandmother."

"You're a novice, child," she says. "Souls are slippery things. They may take on all kinds of forms, or characters that bear little resemblance to the bodily form they once inhabited. We can't use a person's medical notes, photographs, or biography, to locate the *right soul* during the retrieval process. The shades of the afterworlds are impressions, not actual embodiments of people and it's impossible to predict exactly what, or whom, you'll encounter."

"I know all that," I say. "This is my twenty-first time, an important occasion for a soul chaser and symbolic of the twenty-one grams of hope we bring back from the retrieval procedure. I want this occasion to be special as my first rite of passage in our calling and I won't let you make this *ordinary* for me."

"Your *attitude* is risky."

"I understand the rules. Even the 'cleanest' of deaths is complicated by the 'other' agents of human multicellularity, which compete with the ego of the deceased for organisational dominance within the decomposition landscape. I also know the *wrong soul* can be brought back, leading to severe identity crises, insanity and tragically, even suicide."

"Child, this is a different scale of difficulty altogether. Nobody has experienced the level of chaos you are likely to encounter in this decomposition landscape. The whole thing is an *experiment*. Heavens, even recognising *yourself* will be far from straightforward."

"I know *you'd rather be doing this*, Grandmother. But you can't."

She grunts and flicks her finger across the screen several times.

"This is unknown territory, child. The causalities will not be linear. Things will appear to happen back to front, the wrong way around, or completely out of place. You'll have to work very hard to navigate this decomposition landscape and while I don't think you're skilled enough, the precedent for this research is an important one."

"What's that?"

"We need to learn how to properly retrieve souls from 'chaotic' environments, which is a particularly important issue for compound trauma."

"Then, *help* me, Grandmother to one day, be as accomplished as you are."

"Sniff," says Grandmother as she straps me into the retrieval chair. I hate this bit.

"Sniff. *Now,*" she says poking a blood-filled dropper with samples from the deceased into my left nostril. "They're about six hours away from reanimation."

I breathe the puff of stems cells sharply in, like snuff. They sting the back of my throat. My eyes are streaming.

"I forbid you sneeze," says Grandmother. "This concoction is only paid for once."

The surgical spotlight gnaws my retina as she trims smooth my shaven my head with a laser and slaps on the jellied skull cap. After some fine tuning, her pitiless pupils scour the electrical connections, ensuring that skin contact is faultless.

"Remember the principles of retrieval," she says.

I nod, as the grips on my wrists and ankles snap shut and the tongue-clamp is inserted.

"Biting down gives you greater control," she says. "It helps you let go of your fondness for life. Try to bring *everything* back. The older you are, the harder it gets to let go of the attachments formed during the retrieval processes. This makes us crazy – so, you can only bring back *one* soul."

Mortazepam scours my veins. I clench my teeth.

"Wait for the *right time*, child, before you retrieve the *right soul*," she insists. "Death is a surprisingly slippery thing."

"What do you mean?" I wonder, with a bit in my mouth.

"Up until the 1950s, child, a person was pronounced dead when any of their vital functions ceased – the heartbeat, electrical brain activity, or respiration. Each organ system was thought to be dependent on the others and it was believed that if one collapsed the others would perish along with it, just like dominoes."

Grandmother's pressing firmly on my scalp, plotting the form of my brainwaves against my cognitive function. I do my best to follow her.

"When effective cardiopulmonary resuscitation techniques were invented, they could keep the blood flowing for up to around forty minutes after the heart had stopped beating with no lasting brain damage, but they could not reverse a stopped pulse. If the formal heart rhythm did not spontaneously return, then medical intervention was needed. In other words, a new diagnosis of *circulatory death* became possible."

"So, people could be brought *back from the dead*."

"Some were revived, but more importantly, whole new classes of people that were neither fully alive nor dead existed. The diagnosis of *brain death*, where bodies in a suspended state of existence, with no measurable brain activity, warm bodies and circulating blood, were made possible by artificial ventilators, and were lively enough to fight off infections, or even gestate a baby."

"So, people could metabolise without truly 'living'?"

My lips are numb. I cannot be speaking.

"Correct, and death becomes even stranger still, child, with advances in organ transplantation, where brain-dead donors are ideal sources for multiple organ harvests. People can now be part-resurrected, or even harbour multiple identities following the retrieval process. In some cases, when human tissue is cultured, individual cells can outlive the donor's body and be part of an independent new life."

Grandmother always manages to make the task ahead seem straightforward, or maybe this clarity is because of the *mortazepam* in my veins.

"You are entering a highly contested territory, child, where new organs are being actively grown inside a catastrophically damaged body, whose flesh is deeply contaminated by environmental microbes. All kinds of human and nonhuman agents will be vigorously competing for control over this resurrection process."

"I'll be careful."

"You'll need to be smart. Some beings will only have the loosest associations to the material realm. Our irresistible life force makes us especially vulnerable to these parasites. They'll grasp at your presence like burrs, if you let them, cling to you, weigh you down, and drive you mad." Grandmother tugs on my lower lids. "Look up!" she says.

As much as I loathe this prodding and poking, clipping and pinning, there's no point arguing with her. She's had so many telomere repair therapy sessions that, in everyday terms, she's *ancient* and equally wise.

"When you enter the decomposition landscape, be mindful of where you are and who's around you. Don't get lost."

"Of course not."

The apparatus starts to twist around me, and my skin tightens from whatever *else* she's just given me, *corpsedrine*, I suppose.

"Watch out for vagrant spirits," says Grandmother, as the chair folds me into its panels, wires and screens like a boa constrictor.

Grandmother slips on her own headset and introduces metal braces, like a Jew's harp, between her teeth.

"Stay alert," she says.

I can't answer her. The *mortazepam*, *corpsedrine* and whatever else she's given me, are really taking hold. My mouth is slack, and I know I'm drooling. I always do.

"The *right soul* at the *right time*," she says, emphasising our fundamental doctrine.

Travelling

I'm being sucked out of my body, passing through my grandmother's huge eyes into a kaleidoscope of forms. Then, I'm squirted through the scalp electrodes into the decomposition landscape of the deceased – a partly decomposing, partly regenerating tissue culture that is organising around me.

Liminal

"Can you hear me, child?"

Grandmother is out of focus. Her words break on the shores of meaning and spill into the liminal realms of my thoughts.

There are no facts.

Freed from my own bodily ties, I am little more than a vaporous presence, carried by an electronic ether. Searching for remnants of nerves and muscles, I start to travel through the decomposition landscape, as sense falls apart.

"Establish the apparent sense of the situation, child," says Grandmother, whose lightless gaze draws into focus.

I *feel them* first.

Vagrant souls draw closer to my presence, bringing me into proximity with odd fragments of reality, partial narratives, corruption, marginal occurrences, the monstrous and other disgusting aspects of existence.

Something's tugging.

"I've made contact, Grandmother."

Barrows

"Where are you, child?"

"I'm approaching a bungalow in Ringlestone, on the outskirts of Maidstone. The whole site is unstable, feeding on memories, fictions and half-truths."

"What *kind* of place is it?"

"It's tired, dull. There is so little here on offer here for the council estate residents. The most generous feature is an arcade of sole-trader grocer shops, which peddle granulated coffee, long-life milk, gritty tea bags, suffocated pastries, processed cheese inseparable from its plastic coating, crustless bread, margarine, a range of sauces and other condiments. Only the truly impoverished would support this dismal place."

"Does it speak to you?"

"Nothing but deception and lies, Grandmother. Once the town was set to flourish alongside an extended 'Chunnel' rail service that linked international centres, like London and Paris, but a morbid fear of 'foreigners' put an end to such prosperity. As pensions are almost worthless, clouds of betrayal lurk at every non-functioning bus stop, closed post-office and silent community centre. Those who live here are simply marking time, until they move somewhere else, or die, but there's a stronger signal now."

"Where is it coming from?"

"Further along the A229, somewhere around Bluebell Hill, which is on the North Downs. There's a shady wood here, which blooms with carpets of blue flowers in the springtime and is teeming with Adonis Blue butterflies, Silver-spotted Skipper butterflies, Black-veined moths, Fiery Clearwing moths and Straw Belle moths."

""The dead are drawn to such vibrant places, child. Are there any signs of the afterworlds?"

"Kits Coty is making itself known, an ancient burial site made up of two distinctive mounds. The first of these is Kit's Coty House, a barrow made of sarsen stone, while the other is Little Kit's Coty House that is made of a tight cluster of twenty sarsens called *the Countless Stones*, lying flattened like tipped dominoes around the remains of a burial chamber. The whole decomposition landscape here is extremely restless."

"Take care child. These ancient grounds are invigorated by the site's historic confluence of highways, which attracts desperate ghosts set loose into the world by trauma. Playing out their personal tragedies time upon time again, they seek reincarnation at any cost."

Notice us.

"They're already here, Grandmother. I'm moving away from their negative energy and making my way back up towards the hill. The whole site wants to speak."

We're watching you.

"Whenever a place has something to say, child, tragedy is not far away."

"The hillside is drawing my attention to spectres of unusual *accidents* in this area. The emotion is intense."

"Trauma is itself, a phantom, child."

"Before me are the astonished faces of Ian Sharpe, and Chris Dawkins. Both are driving home late at night when, without warning, a young, fair-haired, woman steps out in front of them. Dressed in white, she momentarily stares at them before they collide."

She stopped and looked at me. There was no expression on her face.

"What singles out these events?"

I thought I had killed her because it wasn't as if she were see-through or anything. She was solid – as real as you are.

"They're part of an unusual and persistent pattern of tragic traffic accidents along the hill. There's more here. Another driver, Maurice Goodenough, a bricklayer from Rochester, also hits a little girl, so he stops for her."

It was a hell of a bang.

"He finds the child, around ten years old with shoulder-length brown hair, wearing a lacy white blouse and white ankle socks. She is on the ground, moving her head and asking for her mummy. He tries to flag down passing traffic, but nobody stops to help. Thinking it unwise to move her without medical assessment, he covers her with a blanket and speeds off to Rochester Police Station to report the accident. Thirty minutes later they return to the scene, but only the blanket remains. Although they raise a search party and look for her with tracker dogs among the wooded cover of the chalk bank, no signs of bloodstains or an injured girl, are found."

We would appeal for any parent whose child has some unexplained injuries like a bump on the head to contact us. We would also like to hear from anyone whose child is missing.

"Are there many of these ghosts?"

"Plenty. Around twenty other female spectres – from young women in dressing gowns to hideous hags with piercing black eyes and cavernous jaws. All are asking for lifts late at night from drivers at various sites along the A229.

"Why is the site disclosing these tragedies now?"

"It wants the *ghosts of Blue Bell Hill* to be actual events, not fables, so their tragedies can be mourned and forgotten."

"When produced by existential trauma, such scars on the landscape can last indefinitely, child."

"When the phantoms are reported to the police, Grandmother, the hill considers them real, and therefore, resolvable."

Who is she?

"Is the site indicating any particular tragedies, which trigger the transition from fable to reality?"

"It's showing me a tragic car crash in 1965. Suzanne Browne is on the way home from her hen party in her Ford Cortina with her friends Judith Lingham, Patricia Ferguson and Gillian Burchett. Colliding with a Jaguar travelling in the other direction near Lower Bell on Bluebell Hill, Judith is killed outright, while Patricia Ferguson and Suzanne die some hours later at the West Kent Hospital. Gillian tells the authorities that she warned Sue about two dazzling lights approaching and that they would be run off the road. She remembers nothing after that."

Who is she?

"What of the phantom child?"

"At times, it seems the-bride-to-be is the ghost that troubled Ian and Chris, causing them to report their sightings to the police and so bring the ghosts of Bluebell Hill into the media spotlight. At other times, Judith appears to be the phantom. Grandmother, I don't think this place actually knows who she is. The whole place is deeply traumatised."

Where are they going?

"Take care, child. These traumas reach far into the decomposition landscapes. We are likely to see many manifestations of this shade – or shades – yet to come."

"But if I can't be sure who the spectres *actually* are, then how do I find the *right soul*, Grandmother?"

"Pay much closer attention, child. The afterworlds are deceptive. To find the *right soul*, you must stay vigilant to the turn of events – in more sites than just this one."

"But… I don't understand."

"Hush, child. Can you feel *something* now?"

"Yes. *Someone* is pulling on me. They're drawing me backwards away from the hill and towards the Ringlestone estate. Keep me safe, Grandmother. This is an unusually strong soul."

Hole

Winifred Lane sits down in her bungalow on the Ringlestone estate for afternoon tea, which she takes in a proper china cup and saucer that keeps it hot.

A horrible clatter outside disturbs her peace.

"Whatever are those builders at number 47 up to now?" she mutters.

She's surprised that the workmen have still not put down their tools when it's been raining so steadily, the place ever drearier than usual. Carefully placing her tea on a cotton doily, she decides to investigate and wipes both hands on the very large pockets of her nylon household pinafore.

A selection of dog-eared popular science books is piled in the corner: *What is Life? Earth's Origins; The Inner Life of Trees* and *The Brain – a Quantum Computer.* She rises incredibly slowly on account of the pain in both her hips and knees, but her shoulders are strong. Being in a hurry, she does not reach for her Zimmer frame, but furniture-climbs her way along the hallway. Scuffing the carpet like a scrubbing brush with her sheepskin slippers, she makes her way down the hall. Breathless, she undoes the deadlocks at the top and bottom of the frame and pushes the door wide open to get a clear view.

It's drizzling as usual, but the whole front lawn and pathway has disappeared, along with her waterproof-covered mobility scooter. In its place is a gaping sinkhole into which a stream is musically trickling.

Holding on to the doorframe with both hands, Winnie peers down into the hole and, feeling very giddy, realises she cannot see the bottom.

Hitchhikers One

"How did we get caught us up in this mess?" Winnie asks the young woman.

"Shhhh," she pleads, "he'll hear you."

A third woman on the back seat snores loudly, rolling her face over

Will's books, and wakes herself up.

She glares at the young woman and says, "He can't hear *us*. He can't see *us* – but he *can* see and hear *you*."

I'm here to teach you a lesson.

"Oh no!" says the young woman, "I was hoping *you'd* gone."

She covers her ears and turns her back on everyone.

Two Tribes

"This is a messy landscape, Grandmother. I've never come across a place that's so contaminated by *other things*."

"None of us are pure expressions of essence or form, child."

"What are we, then?"

"Strangely choreographed entanglements produced by myriad bodies, linked through deep time."

"The *soul* is pure, Grandmother."

"Nonsense, it is an expression of these same co-habiting agents."

"What about the *right soul?*"

"Souls are inextricably interwoven with and by the community of life, child. If we go back to life's origins, where the first creatures simmered upon the surface of warm little ponds, and smouldered in the belly of geothermal black smokers, ecosystems of interdependent metabolic bodies set the scene for multicellular life."

"Did they have souls, Grandmother?"

"Not as we presently recognise them, but they did have a unique life force. This *proto-soul* was shaped by two distinctive types of creatures that dominated the early Earth. On the one hand, bacteria used their incredible powers of metabolism to rapidly multiply, adapt and respond to every condition the world could throw at them. Adept at weaponising their survival, they invaded and colonised all kinds of niches. This remarkable ability to transform the world was earned at the expense of structural complexity. By forming colonies and biofilms, bacteria *pretended* to be multi-cellular creatures, and in *pretending to be* a complex organism, they dreamed and built a kind of soul together."

"What were the other creatures?"

"Archaea, which are also ancient microorganisms. Rivalling bacteria in their metabolic diversity they are *also* able thrive in extreme environments, but their abilities are shaped by creativity and kindness. Embracing each other so fondly, they began to internalise each other through multiple acts of swallowing and partial ingestions. Over aeons, they became morphologically inventive, engulfing each other, as well as bacteria, through multiple acts of love, lust and care. These manifold creatures created the possibility of multicellular life with the kind of fully formed souls we recognise today. These eukaryotes also include 'humans'.

"Are you saying we're *entirely* descended from microbes?"

"Of course. People exist because their forbearers were palimpsests, manifolds, and mixologies of many kinds of nonhuman beings. Their life-force has survived and evolved throughout deep time, way before our hominid ancestors emerged. Our common thread of survival rests on our capacity to embrace each other. Many small fundamental acts of inclusivity have allowed us to be *more than* what we once were. As our souls have evolved together, so has the attraction between them, which has led to our capacity for empathy and our affinity for those that are *not like us*."

"Then, how are we unique?"

"People are not special in a singular way such as our individual genetic make-up, or brain function but rather, because we are engulfed and enfolded within other beings. This is not purely about our archaeological traces of viruses and bacterial signatures within our genomes but also our ongoing symbiosis with our human microbiota."

"They're inside us, Grandmother. They're not *part* of us."

"Indeed, they are. Colonising the most intimate surfaces of the human body, our microbes are an integral part of our function. They work like an organ, helping us digest food, making mood-elevating substances, forming a first line of defence against marauders and even producing oils that make the skin supple. They are so entangled with our health and identity that not only do we share our physical well-being with them, we are also empathetically entwined."

"If we're indistinguishable from microbes, then how am I ever going to find the *right* human soul, Grandmother?"

"I didn't say we are indistinguishable. When a body dies, it becomes increasingly microbial, so its value landscapes change. Just remember that in the decomposition landscape, *nothing* – or *nobody*, is entirely human."

Hitchhikers Two

"Excuse me," says Winnie. "I don't know what your issues are, but I suggest that, in this rather confined space, we make a wholehearted effort to get along with each other.

Anne casts her a long look.

"You're a bit of a busybody, aren't you?"

"Since there's no telling how long this journey is going to last," says Winnie, "let's have a round of introductions. Why don't you go first?"

Inexplicably, the fractious woman falls suddenly fast asleep.

The young woman remains curled up on the seat, arms over her head.

"Well, how rude," says Winnie, but since there is nothing else to do, she waits for one of them to awaken.

Persistent Imprints

"Are ghosts *real*, Grandmother?"

"They are physical traces of souls that have been set loose into the world by trauma, but they are not *fully* material. Arising at the moment profound distress shears the life-force from a living body, they try to reinvent their lot by allying with sorts of matter and unlikely bodies in the search for happily-ever-afters and never-agains. When this fails, they pit their fury on the living."

"How is a spirit different to a ghost?"

"Spirits are entirely ephemeral beings that are loosely attached to living things, acting upon their thoughts and imaginations. Souls, however, are denser and penetrate organismal matter, released only through the territorial contest between different agencies at the moment of death. While all manifestations of the afterworlds can be benevolent, malign ones seduce our living souls, cling to them and feed upon their energy, making them so weak they can never be reincarnated."

"Are they dangerous?"

"Unhappy phantoms are desperate things and if they see you as a path to reincarnation, they'll never let you go."

"What if I come across one?"

"They are devious entities. Only the strongest souls can overpower their unhappiness unaided; however, the life-bearing force of flowing water can also purge them from reality.

"How is that possible?"

"It causes them to temporarily, collapse like antimatter, which loosens their hold on a victim. We don't know how effective this is, so be on your guard, child."

Hitchhikers Three

"I'm a geologist," says Anne, as if she'd been awake all the time.

"I didn't ask *what*, I want to know *who* you are?" says Winnie, using her elbows to defend some personal space from this seat-spreader.

"Oh, I've many names," she says, somewhat too cheerily, "but I prefer Anne," and forces her upper lip to curl into a smile.

"Get lost," says the young woman on the back seat, refusing to engage in pleasantries.

"So, now we're all *here*, in this purgatory," says Winnie, "let's find civil ways to keep ourselves occupied."

I know what you're here for.

Anne smirks.

"You say you're a geologist," continues Winnie. "Why don't you tell us something about your practice? We may as well try to learn something while we're here."

"I take a rather *unconventional* view of the subject," says Anne.

"I expect nothing less," says Winnie.

"My art embraces the mythical dimensions of conventional science."

"What on earth does that even mean?" asks Winnie.

"I study the deepest secrets of life."

"Such as?" asks Winnie.

"The Earth is an igneous egg," says Anne.

"An *egg*? I'm pretty sure that's a first for a *geology* discussion."

"I choose my words carefully. This egg is not an ordinary object. *Stupid people annoy me.*"

"Well, you may as well enlighten me," says Winnie, wrinkling her nose. "I'm quite an aficionado of unusual *facts*."

We're watching you.

"The outer layer of the egg, of course, is the shell. You might know it as the Crust, which is mostly covered by water, sand, clay, soil and ice. Reaching a thickness of around thirty-five kilometres over the continents, it tapers down to around seven kilometres at the ocean floor."

"That's not a secret," says Winnie. "*Everyone* knows that."

"Patience. The next layer is equivalent to albuminous egg white, which you might recognise as the Mantle. Made up of a layer of silicon, oxygen, aluminium and iron, it is around three thousand kilometres deep."

"I applaud your use of metaphor," says Winnie, "but I really don't think you're saying anything new."

"Don't interrupt," says Anne. "Beneath this is the yolk, made of fiery brimstone, liquid nickel and iron. You'll know this as the Earth's Core."

"Of course. It's the origin of geothermal events."

"Right," says Anne, "and you'll also know that eggs are structures for creature-making."

"Sure," says Winnie.

"What you won't know, is that plasma blindworms are constantly birthed from this yolk."

"Sorry, what – worms?"

Anne's outrageously curly hair won't lie against her scalp and her layers upon layers of clothing appear to be actively multiplying. Goodness knows how many frocks, knickers and vests this woman has on.

"*Plasma blindworms.* They're a unique species of cosmic lizard that are born without legs, or teeth. Leaping in lava, burbling at the base of geothermal vents and animating the tectonic plates that compose the Ring of Fire, they are constitutionally irritable, provoking quakes, setting the periodicity of geysers and stirring the wrath of tsunamis."

"Steady on," says Winnie. "You're attributing lively geological events to the activities of giant... *worms*."

"*Plasma blindworms*," insists Anne.

Winnie shakes her head slowly, watching the woman's tiny pupils squeeze to almost nothingness, she is shamelessly making this stuff up.

"Believing that inorganic life is the most elegant expression of matter, plasma blindworms seek to return the Earth to its primordial state."

"They want an entirely volcanic planet?" asks Winnie.

"Of course. To them, the organic world is so rotten, it *stinks*. Instead, they prefer the sulphurous scent of their native realm. So, they stir up the flow of lava, expelling it on to the surface of the living world and transforming organic substrates into fossil fuels, catalysing the return of Earth's the original state.

We're still watching you.

"Well, that doesn't make any sense," says Winnie. "The evolution of this planet depends on the link between the inorganic realm and life. One of the most interesting things I've read is that the mineral realm catalysed the emergence of life by creating new chemical landscapes. These, in turn, allowed new minerals to form. Life begets rock, and rocks beget life. So, the worms are acting against their own interests."

"Exactly," says Anne. "They're quite a paradox."

Messy

"The fractured time-plane is hard to follow, Grandmother. The shades are holding me close and I am losing the ability to place myself at a distance from them."

"Patience, child. This troubled landscape presents existential choices. You must closely observe and establish the meaning of these situations. Malevolent spirits are intruding upon this resurrection."

Grandmother's eyes are always there, as a constant dark moon, calmly holding me in the confusion.

Just as I am tempted to seek more control in the unfolding events, I feel the excruciating chill of a mortazepam bolus.

Overlooked

"I can't believe this. It's a massive hole."

Winnie thinks of walking around the gap to look at the damage from the other side, but it's so big that she can't leave the house.

"Well, this is going to cost a fortune to repair and stops me getting out. How on earth am I going to manage, now?"

She deadlocks the front door and calls the local council.

"It is private land. Nothing to do with us," says the official.

Then she phones Elizabeth next door.

"Sorry, Winnie, but I'm too scared to leave the house."

As usual, her son Jeremy doesn't pick the phone up when she needs him. An unfamiliar woman's voice asks her to *leave a message after the tone*.

"Perhaps, he's seeing someone new," she says. "That would be nice. He has such dreadful taste in women. Or maybe, he's just changed his messaging system."

Finally, she contacts the home insurance agency, who promise that someone will get back to her, but can't say when.

She waits for them patiently. What else can she do?

The glass cabinet that stands by the telephone, stares emptily at her. Inside is a collection of exotic glass beetles that are carefully arranged according to their size. Jeremy sometimes brings her smudgy glassware insects from his travels. Some are remarkably ugly, and others are cast in resin. Winnie tries not to mind that they break her collection rules. It's the thought that counts.

Still, nobody turns up.

Overwhelmed and frustrated by the situation, she sits back down in her armchair and cries quietly as the rain thumps against the windowpanes.

Nobody hears her.

"Alfred would have a reassuring word in a crisis like this," she says to the soggy tissue she stuffs back up her sleeve. "If he was still here, he'd know exactly what to do."

Her best china cup continues to radiate heat, as the tea cools below a palatable temperature. Exhausted, Winnie's head titubates, and she falls asleep.

Surveillance

Will looks for the young woman in the back in his rear-view mirror. Hands over her ears and gentle rocking, is not a reassuring sign. Perhaps it's the shock.

Maybe whoever is expecting her on the other side of town will know what to do.

A giant wave of surface water smashes on the windscreen as an articulated lorry thunders down the A229, oblivious to the treacherous road conditions.

"For crying out loud!" he says. "This is the road to Hell."

Stasis

"Is Winnie the *right soul*, Grandmother?"

"In a chaotic landscape, child, there is no straightforward answer to that question. Everything takes its course. Souls are far more labile in the afterworlds than in a living body, where it is pointless to look for a soul as a complete entity."

"I've been doing exactly that for the last twenty retrievals, Grandmother."

"The rules have changed in this case, child," say her lightless eyes from the darkness. "Souls that appear to be singular are likely to be misleading you."

"I don't follow you, Grandmother."

"Lucid beings within an incoherent landscape are only ever parts of a story, child. Much remains hidden."

"Then how can I retrieve such fragments souls, Grandmother?"

"Healing the fragmented, is not your responsibility, child. Broken souls will find their own coherence through the process of reincarnation. Perhaps in some iteration of their existence, they will finally realise who they *truly* are."

Anti-Rocket Chair

Winnie wakes just as the noise starts.

"What's that rumbling?"

Although she's completely deaf in one ear, the vibrations are so forceful that they wake her bones.

"Maybe I've been snoring. My breathing is not so good nowadays and I can't lie fully flat. I get so out of puff."

Since she's awake, Winnie waits to see if the noise comes back.

"Alf would give me the elbow if I was making a noise in bed. He'd tell me that I breathe so loudly he may as well sleep in a motorcycle garage. He was always poking fun at me. I never really knew whether to believe what he said, or not."

This time the reverberations come up from the ground, travelling right through the roof, and drown out the hammering rain.

She is certainly not snoring now.

The whole room lurches, scattering Winnie's books onto the floor. Then, everything starts to sway.

"Oh, goodness. Am I having a 'turn'?"

Recently, she's been inexplicably weak on the left side, but sometimes the right too. It doesn't last very long but it does make her feel dizzy.

"I can't be. My funny spells only happen when I'm standing, and I'm sitting down now."

The flooring gives way.

As Winnie plummets into complete darkness, she notices, with some relief, that the glass cabinet with its clumsily made insects has been spared and is still attached to a shelf of floorboards.

Accelerating at a brutal speed, her bones and skull start to vibrate like a tuning fork.

"Maybe it's possible to find out how far I'm falling by focusing on a light source." She tries to look upwards but can't lift her neck.

Several seconds into the vicious ride, she thinks of shouting for help, but her face is flapping like a rubber safety bathmat and there is no air in her lungs.

Falling faster still, she rises up and out of her seat, feather-light. Now there is no air in her lungs at all and she's struggling to stay conscious.

After descending for 2 minutes and 42 seconds, Winnie and her armchair come to an abrupt stop, but the old woman doesn't notice it's the end of the ride.

She's still falling towards lightlessness in a flicker of consciousness.

Linking

"Try to make associations between the physical and liminal worlds, child," says Grandmother. "If you let the decomposition landscape lead you, then you'll be faced with an unnavigable space."

"I'm doing my best, Grandmother, but Winnie is taking me through this place *her way*."

Down in the Ground

Spare us the indignity of cremation in toxic ash,
Chemical embalming, extraneous cement, steel
And other non-biodegradable materials. We wish
To live again. Bury us instead, fully fleshed under
The soil in a coffin, so we can become new earth.

Plant a yew tree upon us that drinks us in as
Root-juice. Giving of ourselves to nature, we
Will be restored within ecosystems, our rhizomes
Defending the land as we grow, our fallen leaves
Turning to compost, becoming fertile, sacred ground.

Our dearest won't tend the dead but nurture us.
"Our beloved ones are reincarnated here,"
They will say, "one day, we shall join them within
This charming forest and we will flourish together."

Limbo

Winnie opens her eyes. She is sitting in her armchair. At least, she thinks they are open, but it's pitch black. She looks up to see where she's fallen from but there is no light strong enough to call an aperture. Not even a pinpoint.

"Can anyone hear me?" she calls.

She tries shouting louder but the silence makes her feel remote and more than a little gloomy. To stave off despair, Winnie concentrates on the sounds around her. A steady trickle of water permeates the space, which is hardly surprising, as it's been raining for as long as she can remember.

"It's coming from different heights and into various depths, just like when I used to go walking alongside craggy streams in the countryside with Alf. Before we got old and housebound."

The atmosphere is stifling as there is very little air movement and water continues to trickle in, but there are no obvious draughts to indicate a way out of this place.

"I don't know whether I'm hot, or cold."

She decides to patiently wait for the rescuers and try to keep her mind occupied. She's heard terrible things about people panicking in desperate situations. It never helps matters and inevitably ends in disaster.

"Things could be worse."

After a while the dripping water starts to bother her. The pleasant piano-like tones have become poisonous beats.

"They'll be here soon."

Oddly, her eyesight has not accommodated to the darkness. She doesn't have good vision, but on those many occasions when she's had to feel her way to the bathroom without turning on the light, so as not to wake Alf, there always came a point where even the darkest shadows would turn grey and suggest their form. Yet this place remains completely lightless.

"Maybe the light is being sucked out of my eyes."

She laughs.

"Don't be silly, Winnie, channelling Alf's voice. "You're thinking daft thoughts now."

She remembers to inhale deeply to calm herself, but there's no sound of breathing when she draws breath and no movement in her chest.

The dripping and spilling continue. Winnie finds it hard to remain occupied by cheerful thoughts.

"Perhaps the rescuers aren't coming."

She notices the cave is echoless, which seems odd.

"What if nobody knows I'm gone?"

Her thoughts spiral into cascades of gloom.

"Pull yourself together, Winnie. *Someone's* looking out for you. Jeremy, or Lizzie next-door, will soon raise the alarm."

Thinking positively, however, isn't helping her out of this terrible predicament, but the bad feelings don't make her cry, as they usually do.

"I'm not a sullen person," she says. "Not like that woman Jeremy was seeing. Oh, what's her name. She'd sit with a sour face in the corner of the room not speaking a word. I prefer to stay cheery and get along with everyone. We all get down though. Especially when you're my age."

It takes a few moments to figure out exactly how old that is.

"Eighty-three. Plenty of young ones go before their time but not me. I really can't moan."

Then she considers what she'd complain about if she was going to raise objections to being in this place.

"For starters, I'd fix that dripping noise. It's rather getting on my nerves and there are a number of odd things that can do with sorting out."

She makes a mental note of these inconsistencies, starting with her chair not being wet. Given there is so much water leaking into the hole, this does not seem right.

"I wonder whether, if I wait long enough, the rising water will float my armchair to the surface. Once I'm bobbing around, *someone* will help me out."

It's hard to stay cheery in pitch darkness, as there is so little to orient her senses.

After a while, Winnie's thoughts darken.

"What if I'm the last person alive. Or I'm no longer on Earth. Like Major Tom, gone to space in an armchair."

Fighting back the abyssal thoughts is a losing battle, which begins to chew at her resolve.

"What did I ever do to deserve this?"

She thinks of television programmes that reveal how brave men survived the mental pressures of prisoner of war camps.

"They concentrated on very small things and found joy in them."

Then she wonders why that mattered.

"I don't want to give up on life," she admits. "I may not have lived the best life ever, but it's mine. Who's to tell me what a "good life" is. I'm a *happy person* and nobody can take *that* from me."

Tired of fighting her growing doubts, Winnie decides to explore instead.

"I know it's dangerous," she says. "After all, it is hopelessly dark, and there is a lot of water around. Surfaces will be slippery, and I could fall. If I'm not careful, I could end up in another hole."

Instead of rising, however, she becomes overwhelmed and remains seated.

"Better safe than sorry," she says. "Although things seem bad right now, it could be worse. I once read that when you're expecting to be rescued, it is best to stay where people last saw you. I'll wait for the rescuers to arrive."

Ages pass and she grows impatient.

Abandoning her well-developed streak of common sense, she grips the sides of her chair to push herself up, but she cannot move. In fact, she's completely rigid.

"Perhaps I'm having one of my turns."

She waits, for the stiffness to pass but there is no change. She waits again. Still no change. Realising that she's doing nothing but wait for a rescue that could take a lifetime to come, Winnie drops off to sleep.

Autolysis

"Where is that nauseating dripping coming from, Grandmother?"

"That is the molecular clock of death, child, keeping time for the *thanatobiome* – the ecology of a body's decomposition – which has taken material form in the decomposition landscape"

"What kind of time does it keep, Grandmother?"

"It's marking physiological time, as Winnie passes through the stage of *algor mortis*, when the passive seepages of fluids escape from her membranes, where they were once contained."

"Where does the thanatobiome come from?"

"It begins 'life' as the human microbiota and undergoes a shocking change at the time of death, which leads to a re-ordering of relationships between all the parties that make up the human body."

"When did the countdown begin?"

"At the moment Winne's heart stopped beating and her cells were starved of oxygen. As her blood sunk away from the capillary beds, her corpse took on the silvery hue of *pallor mortis* to experience dreams, voices, visions and strange feelings. As her metabolism expands and slows down, she gradually dissipates into spaces she did not previously occupy, which is an overwhelming, if not terrifying, experience."

"What's causing the oppressive atmosphere?"

"The build-up of Winnie's toxic by-products. As her enzyme-rich liver and watery brain first start to release their contents into her gelatinous body, she becomes a waxen doll-like figurine with black, dilated eyes."

"Oh, that awful sound of dripping again!"

"It will continue for a while, child. All Winnie's tissues and organs are decaying now. Damaged blood cells spill from leaking vessels and, aided by gravity, their iron-rich pigments settle in the capillaries and small veins, discolouring the skin with a gruesome purplish hue."

"Why is she unable to move?"

"That's the onset of *rigor mortis*, where her muscle fibres are locking into a fixed position. The energy source, which once enabled the molecular fibres of her muscles to move over each other like ratchets, has dissipated and will not return. Joints, once supple, now become fixed. Starting in her eyelids, the process spreads down to her jaw, then neck muscles, trickles into her trunk and finally, her limbs. This enforced pause enables Winnie to confront her true nature and explore an alternative identity, which is growing within her transforming flesh and forming a fragile new self."

"What happens to her now?"

"For the first time, her human flesh is merely an object obeying Newton's second law of thermodynamics, rather than a living thing. Everything that she is marches towards an energetically ordered system that is destined to reach a permanent full stop."

"But her soul is so strong, Grandmother."

"That's because stranger things than the classical laws of physics are yet to come, child. While the molecular clock of the thanatobiome is marking the decay of the old woman's corpse, it does not mark time for her alone. There are plenty of other bodies present in this decomposition landscape that can resist the present call to inertia – and they are very much alive."

Sink Hole

A concerned crowd gathers under umbrellas around the gaping hole.

"I heard a terrible crash at number 46," says a concerned neighbour, "but I didn't think the whole house could have gone."

"What's-her-name, must still be inside," says another local, craning their neck in the direction of the hole.

"She'd have died instantly," says the neighbour. "The poor thing wouldn't have stood a chance."

The fire service and police arrive. It's impossible to reach the bungalow as the sinkhole has also destroyed a large section of neighbouring homes. The whole area is cordoned off and the remaining occupants are taken to safety.

"You're not going to put me in an old people's home," says Lizzie-next-door to the two policewomen who are evacuating at-risk buildings by making door-to-door checks of nearby residents. "I've no problems with my health. I am completely independent, and I have all my marbles too. I know what you authorities are like."

"Look, love, this is just a 'routine' safety measure," says the taller officer, noting Lizzie's marked limp and shortness of breath. "It won't be a permanent arrangement."

Eventually, an ambulance crew join the policewomen, who wear Lizzie's concerns down enough, so that she agrees to come with them for "a check-up".

The Kent County Police usher bystanders away from the site.

"Stay away from the edge. There's nothing here to see but eroded soft rock under the house."

Everyone draws in closer despite the ongoing drizzle.

"We're conducting a risk assessment," says a fireman. "You all need to get back. The ground here could give way any time."

Whistling hearing aids scramble the sense of advice from the various authorities at the scene, while those that can hear what is being said, find it very difficult to keep up with the sense of the unfolding events.

"I'm sure I heard the old woman calling out," says an elderly man with ill-fitting dentures. "She must be under the building."

"We'll start the search for her as soon as we can, sir," says the fireman, "but we can't do anything until the rain stops."

The drizzle turns to spittle for a few hours, so rescuers use megaphones to try to establish communication with the occupant of the missing house, but there is no reply.

A wave of excitement ripples from under the crowd's umbrellas as, around an hour later, a swarm of drones with monitoring equipment is released. Dipping like humming birds, they confirm that the occupant is not inside and everything of any significance within the house is gone.

"The kitchen, the bedroom and central corridor have completely collapsed," says the coordinator of Autonomous Rescue Vehicles. "All I can make out is a handful of popular science books and a cabinet full of glass insects, which are tenuously nested on shattered floorboards. The whole site looks more like some weird kind of fly-trap than a domestic building."

At ten the next morning, the police announce a formal change in the programme of events.

"Our search-and-rescue mission is concluded," says a solemn officer. "But we have to wait until the ground is stable enough to retrieve the bodies. It's a tough situation, especially for the family."

Jeremy Lane waits with police as local, then national media, arrive at the scene.

"I'm praying that there's an air pocket in there," he says. "If anyone can survive this dreadful situation, my mother can. She's a tough cookie."

In the hope of getting a three-dimensional image of the sinkhole, engineers turn to more sophisticated equipment, using NASA satellite technology. Although this service is not routinely used by the Kent County Council, it is deemed appropriate for the expanding drama played out across the media.

"Usually, Britain experiences around twenty sinkholes a year," says a

BBC reporter. He is broadcasting live on a news programme in the South East, conducting an interview with Paul Finch, president of *DeepSafe*, an engineering company assisting emergency workers. "However, in the wake of the relentless rain, there have been at least ten in the last month in Kent alone, some of which have spanned more than two metres in diameter. There is no official information about how to tell if one is about to affect your area, or what to do when they happen."

"This hole is expanding," says Paul. "It is currently about ten to fifteen metres across and may be ten deep. Or more. This is not your typical sinkhole."

"Is it a one-off?" asks the interviewer.

"Sadly, these kinds of hazards are becoming more common in the county of Kent. This is the first time a residential area has been so significantly affected. The whole of the Maidstone area lies on bedrock made of chalk and sandstone that can be eaten away by acidic groundwater, or very heavy rainfall. Tiny fissures cause the rock to thin out until it can no longer support the weight of the ground. At that point, it collapses and forms a sinkhole."

"What's the extent of the present problem?" asks the interviewer.

"In the last forty-eight hours a few more sinkholes have appeared along the A229 and have caused serious traffic congestion for those trying to reach the M2 motorway. Previously, this section had been ruined by a five-metre hole in the central reservation a couple of decades ago," says Paul. "Our contractors have already set to work to inject the rapidly appearing holes with high pressure concrete down to depths of around sixteen metres in order to fill metre-and-a-half crevices."

Further interviews reveal the extent of the impact of the geological events that took poor Winnie's home.

"Eight-hour tailbacks have formed," says a traffic police officer and drivers caught in these stationary convoys are only too willing to talk to reporters.

"This whole stretch has hemmed us in between sinking earth and road maintenance machinery," observes a freight lorry driver. "We truckers have been calling this stretch the *Road to Hell*, because the longer we stay put, the greater our chances are of ending up down in the ground."

A strange picture of sodden land crumbling under its residents begins to emerge.

"It's an emergency situation," adds a Gravesend cemetery director. "Families are devastated by a huge number of graves being exposed or swallowed up by the sodden ground. In the meantime, we have closed off areas of the cemetery to the public. Signs outside the cemetery warn visitors to keep off the grass, as in some places, it may only be as thin as a carpet."

"*As Future events cast their shadow before them*, we may wonder whether we're living the *End of Times*," says the reporter.

"It might certainly seem that way," admits a council spokesman. "While it is quite common for graves to sink, especially after a period of heavy rain, nobody has seen anything like this. Not at this scale. It will take some time before our consecrated grounds are restored to their original condition, but there's no need for anyone to panic. We'll be back to rights though, once the rain's done."

Unbound Matter

We are just atoms and particles
That spin around for a while,
Then dematerialise into nothingness:
That's what we're told.
We live awhile and die. Since the soul
Has not been found in laboratory
Experiments; then nothing is said
To survive after death but there are
Critical flaws in this perspective.

When observed, a quantum particle
Will move through one of two slits
Like a bullet, passing through one gap,
Or the other. If unobserved,
The particle behaves as a wave,
Progressing through both gaps
At the same time, *as waves of probability*
That somehow acquire future information
About their nature.

Not confined to the subatomic world,
Quantum weirdness exists at the
Human-scale, defying the classical laws
Of matter, where an aspect of the mind
Exists beyond space and time. This soul,
No less real than a head, hand, cheek or eye,
Shapes our dreams and reality, being bound
To us through the promise of another life.

Plasma Blindworms

"Those *worms* don't make any sense to me," says Winnie.

"*Stupid people* don't understand their complexities," smirks Anne.

"Try me," says Winnie. "I like to figure things out."

The young woman is still curled up tightly in a defensive ball. Winnie can't remember the last time she saw her move.

You need to be taught a lesson.

"What have you to do with *her condition?*" says Winnie. "That poor young woman is definitely trying to shut you out. Even under these peculiar circumstances that doesn't seem *right* to me."

Anne laughs operatically and appears to grow several dress sizes as she speaks.

"You are so preoccupied with trivia that you can't see the epic scale of the events unfolding around you. But since you asked about the intricacies of the plasma blindworms, I will begin with their mating ritual."

"I trust your biology is better than your geology," says Winnie.

"After lying head to head in a continuous circle with the male, the female lays her eggs deep within the Earth's yolk, ensuring an entirely self-contained existence for the developing embryos, which have no need for eyes, ears or organs."

"What makes you think they exist at all?" says Winnie.

"Oh, they exist all right," says Anne, "but *someone like you*, of course, wouldn't notice."

"Whatever does that mean?" says Winnie.

"*Ordinary* people can't endure the aeons of slow development it takes to mature a worm. To reach a complexity and scale when passive forces alone can no longer sustain them," says Anne. "It's a tragic situation. To survive, they must destroy the perfect peace and symmetry of the interior environment of their eggs and make their entry into the world's contaminated surroundings."

"How might *someone like me* notice them?" says Winnie.

Why are you even alive?

"Through geological events. After hatching, the plasma blind worms stay deep inside the Earth, where they suck up nickel and iron through their boneless flaming mouthparts. Reaching temperatures that are as hot as the surface of the sun, they constantly stir the Earth's Core, forming currents and magnetic eddies. Here, they generate the circulation of magma under the surface of the world upon which the giant stone ocean floats to produce the planet's plate tectonics."

"I've got to hand it to you," says Winnie, observing how the young woman is curled hand to toe like an ouroboros. "You're perplexingly patronising. What makes you think I wouldn't notice an earthquake?"

"Oh, even the stupidest person would notice a big tremor, but it takes a special kind of sensibility to observe and read the constant, nuanced vibrations they produce."

"Right," says Winnie. "I'm really not sure what you're adding to the topic of geology. While your ideas are intriguing, they are also absurd. Nothing is *right* about *anything* you say."

"I don't expect you to understand," says Anne, "but since you asked for a lesson, know these worms are extraordinary, but not harmless."

"Really," says Winnie.

"They *hate bodies that smell* of organic matter and uncompromisingly patrol their territory, especially the young ones, who are least familiar with the stench of life. As they stalk the ground beneath us, they seek every opportunity to prevent the most potent expressions of the organic realm – living or dead – from flourishing."

Winnie doesn't like how Anne smiles through cold eyes.

Part II - Decay

Lust

Winnie stands up.

"Stop your gurgling, stomach," she says, "I don't feel the least bit hungry."

As she's usually desperate for a cup of tea and biscuit after taking a nap, this surprises her.

"Well, that's odd. I haven't felt *this* good since long before I wound up in this place," she says. "Even the pains in my knees and hips have gone."

She sits down again just to check that she's not imagining things, then stands up, pain free as before.

"Maybe I could make the most of sitting and rising, without my usual aches, while I wait for the rescuers."

After a while, the excitement of being pain free isn't enough to stave off the creeping feeling of abandonment.

"I'd better resort to *plan B*," says Winnie. "If I got in to this place, then there has to be a way out again. I'll be careful, though this whole situation is more than a little odd."

She pushes off from the sides of her armchair, feeling the warp and weft of the ribbed polyester and cotton cloth upholstery in amazing detail through her hands. Tiny channels of still air are trapped with the fabric like freshly ploughed rows of thread and – *something's moving*!

Winnie rapidly pulls her hand away, recoiling from the prospect of creepy crawlies and freezes, waiting for something horribly strange to happen, but all is quiet.

After a while, she makes light of her overreaction.

"Typical me, to be nervous around things that move. I was always the first to jump on to the chair when there was a mouse around," she says. "Alf would run about with a heavy shoe, while I pointed to its whereabouts. Eventually, we'd lose sight of it, or the *poor thing* would be flattened. Either way, we'd end up falling around, laughing at our antics."

Soon she realises that her feet are just as sensitive as her hands. Even with her sheepskins on, she can sense the ground's texture beneath her. It's soft and slightly spongy, but not like soil. More like sandstone. A scattering of grit spills from somewhere above onto her pinafore and she brushes it off. The tiny grains feel like marbles.

Feet and fingers as eyes, Winnie scuffs her way along in the complete darkness. Taking cautious steps, she reaches into the space in front of her with outstretched hands and feet, anticipating a collision. The wisp of a current blows gently on her left and she inches her way towards it.

"Maybe this is the way out?"

Finding a dank wall with an irregular pattern of troughs and peak, like tiny teeth to guide her.

"Maybe, it's a special kind of Morse code," she says, "but I can't make any sense of their patterns."

She draws back. A large feathery body just moved over her hand.

"Calm down, Winnie, you're overreacting."

She doesn't want to think about what it might be, but she can't get rid of the impression that it had hundreds of legs.

With considerable urgency, she presses her palm against the rock face, trying to find some detail that suggests an opening, and discovers an oddly geometric crack. Exploring its contours in more detail, she establishes it's a doorframe and searches for where she thinks the handle should be.

Finding a doorknob, she twists. Mercifully, the door is not locked. As she carefully pushes it open, tiny limbs brush past her hand again, but she's not worried now, as she's entering another room.

Hitchhikers Four

"Your *geology* and your *biology* are complete rubbish," says Winnie.

"I'm unorthodox, *you, ignorant woman*," says Anne as she sprawls over the seat and instantly falls asleep.

"Its rude to take up all of the seat," says Winnie "That goes for both of you."

The young woman remains curled up next to her, holding her head.

Anne begins snoring horribly and since Winnie can't rouse her, she peering through the smears of light that spread like butter over the window and leak into the darkness.

"Sometimes the rain makes ugly things seem almost beautiful," she says.

Thanatobiome

"Brace yourself, child," says Grandmother. "A new tipping point of order in the system has been reached."

"What is happening?"

"Chaotic patterns are forming, within the decomposition landscape, child."

"Should I be worried?"

"Expect sudden change, child," says Grandmother. "Winnie's body is succumbing to the appetites of bacterial invasion as her microbiota become the thanatobiome, Unchecked by her immune system, the thanatobiome she is becoming is gluttonous to a fault. Running amok in every organ, it reorganises her flesh and desecrates her integrity from the inside out."

"Can she maintain her identity, Grandmother?"

"Impossible, child. Winnie's ego is threated by an orgy of survival and the coordinated activity that keeps her body together is weakening."

"How can we stop this, Grandmother?"

"We can't and shouldn't, child. It's a simple question of nature and numbers. Bacteria are the most prolific breeders of all organisms. Exchanging intimate secretions, entwining each other's genes and whispering the erotic languages of the cellular realm, they multiply so vigorously that familiar anatomical boundaries are breached. Crazed by unlimited possibility, all kinds of microbes now compete for Winnie's enzyme-softened tissues, indiscriminately consuming everything in their path. In the absence of an immune system, the thanatobiome is now free to strike up new relationships with other microbial accumulations beyond the cadaver. With nothing to control their impulses, they even end up inside each other's bodies and swapping all kinds of information. Frankly, some even indulge themselves for the sheer pleasure of it."

"Winnie would blush to be hosting such a metabolic bonfire of lust, Grandmother."

"It's not all bad, child. Her soul is acquiring an inner glow from the strength of the metabolic heat produced by these revellers and is acquiring newfound microbial sensibilities. Now, she has access to a whole range of sensations that do not require vision – like chemical changes, pressure and temperature."

"Is she still human, Grandmother?"

"For now, child. Her thanatobiome continues to cherish the phantoms of its human origins, still acting and identifying as 'Winnie'."

"Even though she's a corpse?"

"Being 'human' is an issue of identification, not materiality. Even in life, she was always outnumbered by her microbiota, child, yet her human life-force dominated her ego. With nothing to civilise the appetites of the thanatobiome, the tipping points brought by unleashed bacterial desires are now the dominant forces that shape her identity."

"Then, what does she become, Grandmother?"

"It's impossible to say right now, particularly as 'other' bodies within this decomposition landscape are vying to forge competing identities and are very different than 'Winnie' the human."

"Oh, Grandmother, how can she persist amidst such depravity? The odds are so very stacked against her."

Crowded

Seven percent of the 105 billion people ever born, are
Alive today. *Behind each person stands fifteen ghosts;*
The ratio by which the dead outnumber the living.
These numbers are dwarfed by the presence of microbes,
Which challenge our numerical sense.
From as low as 120,000 to tens of millions,
Estimates of their species vary wildly.
If all the 1×10^{31} viruses on earth were laid end to end,
They would stretch for 100 million light years,
100 million times as many bacteria
Are in the oceans (13×10^{28}),
As there are stars in the known universe.
The number of microorganisms
In a teaspoon of soil (1×10^9)
Is the same as people currently living in Africa.
The bacteria present in the average human gut
Weigh about 1 kilogram, and each person
Excretes their own body weight
In faecal bacteria each year.
The biofilms that form dental plaque
Are so densely packed that
A gram will contain approximately 1×10^{11} bacteria,
Which is about the same number of people
That have ever lived.

Gluttony

"This must be another home that fell into the sinkhole," says Winnie, feeling her way around a living room, tracing the uneven floor out with her toe before taking a step.

"Perhaps there are survivors."

Feathery fronds coil around her legs.

"Shoo! Go away."

Taking several brisk steps forwards, even more unpleasant gnawing and crunching vibrations come from the centre of the room, so she slowly retreats back through the door.

An overfriendly nose, pokes into her behind.

"Good boy," she says, reassuringly patting the dog as she sidesteps its attentions.

Hot nostrils pursue her as she shuffles quickly onwards.

"Maybe the people who live here need my help," she says, trying not to think about the exploratory sniffing that continues around her crotch.

"At the very least, I could sit with them and keep them company."

She keeps up a good pace, walking in circles around the room, to escape the unwanted attention.

"I could whistle tunes to the people who live here, "she says. "I'm quite good at that. I also like telling stories that cheer people up."

She smiles as she remembers that Alf always said one of the reasons that he 'stuck with her' for so many years, was that she was 'cheerful at heart'.

"*Miserable women* that were always complaining didn't appeal to my Alf," she says, "but when you read as much as I do, there's no time to be unhappy. There's always another book and another set of interesting facts to take your mind off any worries."

Winnie's shins suddenly meet the edge of a sofa or armchair cushion. More noses poke themselves into her. The crunching vibrations are forceful here. Keeping her hands outstretched to try and defend at least a modicum of body space from the dogs, she walks quickly backwards.

"Good dogs," she repeats as she retreats from the intrusive snouts and hot breath, "I'm not trying to hurt you."

One jumps up at her.

Instinctively turning her back, she grabs the sofa to steady herself. Her hand touches what feels like a body part; a leg.

"Someone's lying down," she says, snatching her hand away. "Maybe they're sleeping. It's so hard to see. I wish someone would turn on a light."

Reaching back in the direction of the person, she finds the end of a boot and feels upwards along the shin to try to locate its owner.

"There's not one, but two people here," she says. "They're entwined in an embrace."

Finding a face, she tries to establish which body it belongs to and feels an irregular, wet cavity rupturing the smooth skin contours.

"Oh, my goodness, some flesh is missing."

Winnie wipes her hands on the front of her pinafore. Having already inadvertently touched these poor people, she decides to assess the extent of these injuries and finds open wounds on the head, neck and hands of this person.

"How dreadful. All the exposed body parts are horribly damaged."

Rough fur pushes against her. She feels for the other body and its injuries are just the same.

"Good gracious," she says. "These dogs must be chewing on the remains of these people, who probably once considered themselves as one big happy human-dog family. I thought a dog would sooner starve than eat its dead owner, but I guess an animal is an animal."

She takes a step back from the horrid scene, remembering that back up on the estate, Bessie from number 31 had a pampered poodle that had to be taken away.

"It made such a mess of her diabetes-damaged feet that they had to be amputated. Apparently, her toes were so numb that she couldn't feel her pet gnawing on them."

One of the noses starts to lick her leg. Its extreme heat is slobbering on her and she quickly draws back, too quickly.

"Calm yourself, Winnie," she says, "dogs know when you're afraid of them."

Although she maintains her composure, she can't supress terrible stories about people being eaten by dogs from intruding on her thoughts.

"I can't help but think of poor Jezebel's dreadful end. Of course, this is a story from the Bible. We don't have a Jezebel on our estate. If I remember correctly, she was thrown over her balcony dressed in all her finery at the command of General Jehu for blasphemy. Trampled by horses and eaten by dogs, her remains ended up at the walls of the city, where the trash was dumped."

It's a sickening thought.

"Good dogs."

The noses start growling.

"Don't run, Winnie, you'll invite an attack."

Moving slowly backwards, she rolls up the corner of her pinafore into a thick cushion, in case she needs to use it to fend off snapping jaws.

The unpleasant feathery feeling returns, circling her ankles.

Oddly reassured by this gesture, she follows it towards a thin draught creeping over the floor without turning her back on the dogs. Feeling for the doorframe, she cautiously turns the handle and backs out of the room.

Ring

Will's ring is biting down on him. He tries to loosen it but can't. Taking one hand off the wheel, he uses his teeth to pull it from his finger, but to no avail.

"How odd. It's become a part of me," he says.

Where Do We Go Now?

Once we're dead, our tissues become fluid.
Like glass, transitioning between liquid and
Solid states, becoming more rigid, ordered.
From the outside, we are symmetrical
But our innards are skewed, caused by
Flow instabilities; the heart on one side
The liver on the other. Sometimes our
Skin spreads out like a tablecloth and
Like Narcissus, we trace its memories
Through the lineaments of our faces,
Back to the nature of our rotten bones.

Flows

"It's hard to keep my bearings, Grandmother."

"You're letting these souls get too close to you, child. Keep a safe distance from them."

"The more I try to separate from them, the closer they draw me in."

"Then you must adjust your attitude towards them."

"How?"

"Give these souls less reason to feel secure around you, but don't let them stray too far, or they will bleed into their surroundings and disappear altogether."

"They tug at me so persuasively, Grandmother."

"Stay focussed, child. The native ecologies of the afterworlds have no innate rhythm, and it is far too easy to mistake your affinity with a soul, for real insights about its nature."

Hitchhikers Five

"*You'll have to face up to what you did,*" Anne says to the young woman.

"That's enough," says Winnie. "Why are you tormenting her – and in *that* condition, too?"

We'll get you in the end.

"This is none of your business." Anne laughs forcefully.

"It certainly is," says Winnie. "We're here, in each other's space. My problems are now your problems and vice versa. What are you *really* doing here? *She* obviously doesn't want you."

"Oh, but *she needs me,*" says Anne, through narrowed eyes, "And you'd not judge me, if you knew what I've been through."

"Now's as good a time as any to let on," says Winnie.

They glare at each other in defensive silence.

"Penenden's a *blasted* heath," says Anne, with an eerie intensity. "Currently, it's a public recreation ground, about a mile north-east of Maidstone. Maybe you know it?"

Winnie slowly nods, scrutinising Anne's darkening gaze. There isn't much she doesn't know about the Maidstone area.

"You know what," says Anne, as she shuffles up even closer to Winnie. "*That* place, is a thief of souls."

Winnie stares right into Anne's slitted eyes, doubting every word she says. But the strange woman is not waiting for her approval to speak.

"We were tried before Sir Peter Warburton at the Lower Court, in the town," continues Anne.

"Tried?" says Winnie.

"Two of us confessed that we had been in communication with the Devil. Then, Anne Ashby fell into a spate of ecstasy before the bench."

"Good gracious," says Winnie, "trouble certainly follows you around."

"It was a sight to behold," says Anne. "Swelling into a monstrous and vast bigness, she screeched most dolefully. There wasn't a person in the court that wasn't moved."

"That's most distressing, but I really don't believe anything you say."

"The judge asked her if the devil had possessed her at that time," says Anne. "*Stupid people don't understand.* Although she professed that she did not know, the evidence was against her. As she spoke, the Spirit Rug came out of her mouth like a mouse."

"What on earth's a Spirit Rug?"

"A piece of flesh. Ashby confessed to have been given hers by an evil spirit. It was paraded around at the Swan Inn after the trial, for all to see."

"Enough about *others*," says Winnie. "What happened to *you*?"

"I fell pregnant by the Devil."

Winnie takes a deep breath and pats down her 'pinny', searching for words that best express her thoughts on the matter.

"Being full the way I was and all, I expected clemency."

Winnie tries to feel kindly towards the woman but fails.

"Instead, they found me guilty of diabolic heresy. For casting spells and revelling in lustful nocturnal crimes with devils, I was sentenced to death. *You don't deserve to live.*"

For few long moments, Anne is mercilessly dark and substanceless, like a shadow. Except for her cat-like eyes.

"To free myself from this accursed situation, I forced the child from myself with a knife."

"Oh, my goodness, no."

"It was a sacrifice. It was *my* sacrifice – while awaiting sentence," says Anne. "*I stuck the knife in and got it out.* I called upon the Devil to spare me and silence my enemies. In return, I offered him the child's blood."

"Are you even *human?*" asks Winnie.

"You are not my judge, woman," says Anne. "You asked me what I am doing *here*, so now, you will hear it. We walked to the gallows in heavy rain, barely braced for what was to come. Foul weather followed us to the hanging grounds of shame, where the hawthorn was in full bloom. When they accused me by name, I spoke of my sacrifice and cursed all who came to the hanging – *the Devil take your children* – and waited for the demon to come."

A flash of terror flits across Anne's face.

"The clouds grew thick and the sun shrivelled to a pale scar in the sky, but, having given my baby and all away, I was abandoned."

Her expression crumples with hate.

"Then, we stepped up to the gibbet; Mildred Wright, Anne Wilson, Mary Reade, Anne Ashby, Mary Browne, Elizabeth Hynes and me. No demonic saviour came forth to save us, and they hanged us *till our teeth fell out. And I cursed all their unborn babies to death* with my last breath."

Cockle Bread

My baby comes quick, and now is dead,
And we'll go mould some cockle bread.
Up with my heels and down with its head,
And this is the way to mould cockle bread.
Comb me smooth, and stroke its head,
And thou shalt have some cockle-bread.

Scavengers

"I'm afraid, Grandmother."

"Stay calm, child," she says, as I taste the rising levels of mortazepam in my veins. "Try not to let your moral compass unsettle you. Remember, what you are seeing are shades of part-real, recalled and imagined events, not actual things-in-themselves. These souls are leaky and vulnerable to other influences and it's easy to jump to conclusions."

"What *kind* of influences?"

"Mostly environmental ones. Winnie's thanatobiome is expanding again, to become the necrobiome, which includes many creatures other than microbes."

"Which creatures?"

"Oh, mostly beetles, carrion feeders and scavengers that have mastered ways of securing an easy meal that does not have to be chased and killed."

"That's uncivilised."

"Exactly. Under certain circumstances, even our pets are integral to the necrobiome."

"You mean domesticated animals?"

"While feral instincts are curtailed by human owners through complex webs of reward and trust, after they die there is no reason for an animal to uphold any human sense of decency. Nonhumans have different rules and values to us, so when the human presence is no longer the dominant organising force in the relationship, boundaries shift and the rules of interaction change, permeating the decomposition landscape with dread."

"But our pets are emotionally attached to us – and we to them."

"Try to contain your indignation, child. Even domesticated creatures must respect their animal nature. Don't forget, their ancestors scavenged around the outskirts of early human settlements and treated human corpses like any other carrion. While surviving on the rich pickings of our food scraps, the least aggressive creatures befriended early humans and became part of our community and customs."

"Surely, pets don't eat their owners, Grandmother."

"Of course, they do. It's more common than you think. Thousands of people attend casualty departments for dog bites every year, and more than half of those attacks occur at home. On average, there are around seventy-five serious bites for every hundred thousand dogs, with younger victims more likely to be bitten in the face, while older people suffer injuries to the hands and lower body. We see them here in this hospital all the time."

"Those are *accidents*."

"They're a battle of instinct and learning. Although pets *rarely* consume their deceased owners – when they do, it is often under unusual circumstances."

"But that's terrible."

"Distressed animals may vainly attempt to wake their owner, by licking and nipping their face potentially drawing blood, which awakens deep animal instincts and established boundaries are transgressed. In one of our cases, a German Shepherd that welcomed police to the scene of a suicide – a young man who had shot himself in the head – started vomiting skin, hair and other remains shortly afterwards. It is thought that the dog probably went looking for comfort and was unable to refrain from feasting on an abundance of fresh blood."

"Horrible."

"Practical. Hungry animals make the most of what is available to them. When family pets run out of food for prolonged periods it's inevitable that some survive on the remains of their owner."

"I guess so."

"This inevitability also tragically links the fates of pets and their human companions. In another case, a young man who committed suicide by poisoning was found after three days with his head, neck and arm stripped of flesh. Inside the house were also the bodies of his ten cats that had ingested lethal doses of the prescription medicine that he'd taken when they'd fed on his corpse."

"Oh, Grandmother, that's awful."

"It's natural. This kind of confusion in extreme situations is not limited to carnivores but unleashes the full range of animal instincts beyond their 'typical' behaviours. One of the strangest incidents involved the body of an old woman that was found with strange, symmetrical marks on her face. When investigators examined an open drawer, they found a beautifully crafted golden hamster burrow made from human skin, fat and muscle."

"Her pet *hamster*?"

"As scavengers, rodents will make nests within skulls or mummified chest cavities and may line them with hair and human clothing for comfort."

"This is obscene, Grandmother. Winnie can't suffer such indignities."

"Stay focussed, child. Donot let your anxieties force a particular chain of events. Right now, Winnie's thanatobiome has survived a fierce stand-off from the domestic necrobiome, but there are so many other creatures only too willing to usurp her soul's identity."

Greed

Winnie firmly closes the door so that the noses do not follow her.

Beyond it is a space jammed full of people moving in a slow convoy.

"Perhaps, this is the way out," she says, and shuffles into the crowd with some difficulty. Finally, she pushes her way in behind a slow-moving elderly man, where she attempts to stay at a polite distance – but it's hard with all the jostling.

As she trundles along, she notices how self-absorbed everyone is.

While the horde is mostly elderly, a few children scamper here and there, despite the congestion, and unapologetically squeeze between legs.

"Why doesn't that boy help that older woman rather than pushing her?" she says. "He's much more able than she is."

Her objections are swallowed by the strange droning of the crowd.

"Hey, stop pushing from behind," she says, as people at the side of her start shoving in. "Can't you folk in front keep moving? Have you no idea what making an orderly queue means."

She tries overtaking some of the people that, even in her terms, are making a meal of moving slowly. They're all big bottomed with obstructive elbows.

"It's just like when Alf used to try to overtake an articulated lorry on the M25," she says, but soon loses patience with not knowing where she's going.

"Where are we all off to?" she asks politely of a woman of around her age who is jammed up against her and is ignored.

"Since it's so crowded here," continues Winnie, "maybe we should be more considerate of each other's space and try to get along."

Her attempts to bring order to the morass are unheeded.

"How rude, to treat people as if they don't exist."

Then everyone grinds to a halt.

Winnie waits quietly for people to start moving again but she's increasingly anxious about what may be causing the delay. The incessantly trudging feet have turned the ground into a muddy paste. It's uncomfortably squelchy standing still. She's starting to slip and slide and worries that she will fall unless everyone starts moving again. Straining to see what the problem may be, she can see no sign of an actual obstacle. There are no public information systems, no officials around to ask and no indication of how long they may all be waiting.

"This is just like rush hour traffic," she says.

Tempers are fraying in the tailback.

Suddenly, a gammon-faced man with a steely glare, turns on an unkempt-looking youngish woman, who swears loudly as she brusquely pushes through gaps.

"Shut up," he says, repeatedly punching the woman in the head. "You are putting everyone on edge."

She falls to the floor with horrendous injuries, but the crowd doesn't wince. People shuffle into the freshly unoccupied space and the queue reorganizes.

Winnie's too far away to do anything.

"Stop! You can't treat people like that," she shouts, but her protests are disregarded.

She tries moving closer to help the woman up, but she has disappeared somewhere into the sludge.

The man takes up his place again quietly in the gridlocked queue, having effectively silenced his irritation.

Feeling a clump of grass beneath her feet, Winnie reaches down to touch it. It's hair. The whole floor is composed of trampled people, who once fallen, become no more than grapes in a wine press.

"Don't panic now, Winnie," she says. If she stumbles, she'll be mulched into the ground.

A feathery touch strokes the back of her hand.

A large eyeless centipede around a metre long is resting on the shoulder of the person in front of her. Its beating organs are visible through its translucent integument. It runs its unusually long, feathery antennae over her and clatters its sharp mouthparts.

"Delicious."

"I beg your pardon."

"Feed me."

"I will do no such thing. After all, we've not even been formally introduced."

"I'm Cerebus. The great worm. I move through the plasma blindworm tubes from the Movile Cave. The food is so very good down here."

Winnie thinks she's heard about strange worms somewhere before but is confused by what the creature is saying.

"I can't see anything to eat," she says, her appetite curtailed, as being face to face with a giant invertebrate carnivore is somewhat of an appetite suppressant.

"Feed me."

"You said there was plenty of food around."

The centipede moves its feathery fronds intimately over her head and neck. Winnie now understands exactly what this gluttonous creature is after.

"Haven't you just eaten that poor young woman?" she says.

"Too skinny," says the worm. "Feed me."

If she's to avoid becoming slush, or fodder for a giant invertebrate, quick thinking is needed.

"Only if you show me how to get out of here."

Winnie's highly sensitive feet are beginning to make out the shape of macerated teeth, skulls and long bones. The creature passes its antennae over her head again.

"Stop doing that! Do we have a deal or not?"

The worm appears pleased with itself.

"I have a voracious appetite," it says, "which is how I have achieved such magnificent girth."

It belches, and its integument suddenly splits, as if to demonstrate there are no limits to its potential for growth. An even bigger, soft-bodied centipede steps out of the chitin shell, shaking off the membranes that are still attached to its delicate feet, as if it were removing hundreds of pairs of socks.

"Yes, of course we have a deal. I'm ready to grow again. Feed me."

"Not before you tell me who these people are."

"These gluttons are forced to queue in a vile line. It's their own fault, you know. They're motivated by ceaseless acquisition and overindulgence in food, drink, drugs and material goods. You name it; they're in to it. Their lives are centred on consuming things. Of course, these items and addictions never fill the void in their cold, selfish, and empty sensuality. They only care about getting more of something. And they're prepared to wait in line for more of whatever it is they think they need. Anyway, why bother yourself with their welfare. Feed me," says Cerebus.

Winnie feels terribly sad.

"Feed me, I said."

This greedy scavenger is not going to stay quiet. Wondering if she's put anything by, like a biscuit, she rummages in her pinafore pocket. She sometimes stashes treats there, then forgets all about them until she has to remove the slush from out of the washing machine. She hates it when that happens.

Winnie brushes off Cerebus' impatient feathers from her face.

"Leave me alone."

The creature is twirling around at the thought of eating again.

Although her pinafore pocket is empty, Winnie gives nothing away. She can feel a fine white powder at the bottom of both her pockets. There is so much of the stuff she wonders if she's washed the garment with an entire packet of biscuits stashed in each pocket. She grabs a handful of the powder and throws it far into the crowd, hoping that one of the consumers will stomp on the creature it while it's on the floor searching for crumbs.

Cerebus is very quick, and nimble. It devours the titbits even before they've fallen into the muck.

"Delicious."

The creature is whimpering now. Winnie casts the powder further and further into the crowd. Each time she disperses the crumbs, the centipede comes racing back, begging for more. She is quickly running out of this stuff and nowhere near freeing herself from the endless queue – or this dangerous, scavenging worm.

"That's enough for now. Your turn," she says. "Show me the way out of here."

Clattering impatiently, the creature begs for more scraps, but Winnie is resolute. Meeting its inquisitive stare with bold resoluteness, she is all too aware of what the treacherous creature is thinking.

"There are plenty of surprises still in these pockets," she says with absolute conviction, "but if you don't show me the way out of here, you'll never know what you're missing."

Unable to resist a delectable treat, the great worm pushes between the consumers and braces the chain gang of impatient queue makers to make an escape route.

Woman and beast wriggle their way through the body-stomping crowd, slip into a narrow crevice at the edge of the crowd and disappear from view.

Alchemy of Decomposition

"It's so hard to keep track of events, Grandmother. This decomposition landscape is unlike anything I've come across before. What's the trudging? It's revolting!"

"Oh, that's an environmental phantom, child, produced by the decomposition process as Winnie's flesh turns into much simpler material forms. The stomping feet are produced by a variety of abiotic, chemical, or physical forces like hydrolysis."

"What's the strange powder in her pockets?"

"The outer layer of her skin."

"If she's falling apart so rapidly, how does her soul stay so strong?"

"Winnie is now a delectable body composed of many contradictions. Her tissues are actively being broken down by the necrobiome and she is vulnerable to the smallest of disturbances. Needless to say, her identity is unstable."

"Then, I must retrieve her."

"It's not the *right time*. Her dissolution is an inevitable feature of her passage through the decomposition landscape. Make sure you stay at a distance from her. The wrong kind of influence may tip the balance of her fate and suspend her soul within a purgatory of non-identity. If that happens, she cannot be reincarnated."

Pause

The traffic lights bleed green, amber and red across the flooded road. Will checks his mirror before moving safely across the junction, and is concerned that things remain so quiet in the back. The young woman is still curled up on the seat, with her hands over her ears. She's no longer muttering.

"This is a good sign," he says. "Perhaps she's fallen asleep."

Wandering

"I'm confused, Grandmother. This space is so fragmented, and I can find so little to intuitively find my way around."

"You're still a novice, child, and relying too much on the phantom world of illusions to guide you."

"I'm *not* a novice. This is my twenty-first time."

"Then act like an adept. Think with your guts."

"What do you mean?"

"I mean it literally. Instead of 'looking' for sense, sniff and taste your way around."

"That's ridiculous, Grandmother. I'm not a – *dog*."

"Spoken like a true novice. Transformation shapes the afterworlds, which is a deep, material process. Its character is not based on the shapes of light it scatters but the vibrations it produces."

"I can't think *rationally* through *scent*."

"In a place of chaos, such as this, you must first learn to be *receptive*, before you can expect to make *appropriate* sense of its events. You must first lend yourself to the absurd and desensitise yourself to its obscenities. In this way, true knowledge of this realm and what you need to pay attention to, will become apparent."

Vibrations

I'm trying to familiarise myself with the odours and strange oral pleasures of this decomposition landscape, so that I might think clearly through them. First, I conjure forth the aromas of old cheeses, sweaty socks, fish and chip shops, armpits, ashtrays and taverns. Although their olfactory landscapes are delightful, they offer no navigational value.

I try again, with malodorous substances like acetaldehyde, chlorine, ammonia, hydrogen sulphide and putrescine. With persistence, I establish a baseline understanding of these bouquets through their potency, from which I start to orient myself. With practice, I can link my physiological responses with these osmogenes, to understand the nature of things through scent. Seduced by the gastronomical provocations and lingering aftertastes of the flavours of rot, I eagerly indulge their piquant compulsions.

Pinching my nose, I swallow the pungent air.

The most pervasive aromas emanate from the various fractions of crude oil – petrol, diesel, kerosene, turps – which, along with tobacco smoke, characterise human landscapes. Acquiring these visceral thoughts, I am drawn to rotting carcasses rich in putrescine and ammonia vapours, which I instantly recognise as *wurst*, animal fat and salt. Drawing my surroundings inwards, I start to appreciate the intellect of my nose, tongue and palate for the first time. Myriad combinations of flavours settle on my tongue and in the pit of my gut like seasoning, and I perceive the nonlinear strangeness of this place through its many flavours.

Exalted by all that makes my mouth water and nose run, the modalities of decomposition are awakened within me. Ancient senses – smell, taste and touch – that work up close to their subjects, have become inseparable from the more complex ones – hearing, and seeing, which operate at a distance from them. In this realm of rot, there is only one kind of perceiving, where my compound senses are part of an expanded sentient web. My base instincts, feelings and passions can now guide me with renewed vigour and clarity, through this continuously evolving decomposition landscape.

Hitchhikers Seven

"This pregnancy," says Winnie, "how exactly did it *find* you."

"Those that ask the wrong questions, may be *hurt by the answers*," says Anne, who promptly falls snoring and sprawled upon the back seat.

I know they are suffering.

Oh, wake up!" shouts Winnie, shaking her arm, but is unable to rouse her.

"Well, *that's* convenient," she says. "*Everything* about you is *fake*."

The young woman starts rocking and whimpering, still with her hands cupped over her head.

"Does your unspeakable cruelty account for what I suspect is your shameful behaviour towards this young woman?" says Winnie, turning to Anne. "What devious influence do you have over her?"

You're responsible for all this.

Anne opens her eyes, which burn green cuts into Winnie's thoughts. "Check your prejudices, busybody," she says. "When you think *bad things* of others, they *have a way of coming true*."

Anger

"You're taking me to an awful place, aren't you." says Winnie, noting the stench of rotten eggs mixed in with bathroom cleaner all around.

The worm ignores her.

"Oh well," she says, making sure the creature is still within view "I suppose any alternative to the crushing crowd is a good thing.

"It's amazing how I can actually keep up, through," she says, realising that she's been travelling through endless narrow passages at quite a pace behind this treacherous creature. "Despite everything, I'm full of energy."

This doesn't mean the journey has been obstacle-free. Several times the walls have only just been wide enough to slip between, but she's proven lithe enough to negotiate these difficult spaces.

They stop in a warm grotto that echoes with the clatter of the centipede's appendages.

"Feed me."

Winnie throws the creature scraps out of her pinafore pockets and it scurries off after them.

The cave is not hollowed out of sandstone, which formed the substratum of her home, but nests in a limestone terrain. The walls and roof are notched with worm-like casts, while a thermal pool belches out pungent gases.

"What a peculiar place," says Winnie. "It's probably the nearest I'll get to being on another planet."

Beyond the clattering of appendages, she senses the vibrations of fluid steadily trickling through the cave, which suggests it's connected by many underground passages.

"Tell me, is this the way *in* to somewhere, or *out?*"

She reaches down into the pool. The cloudy water is full of impurities, which are mostly sulphurous precipitates. A tenacious film, like the skin that forms on boiled milk that's cooling, floats in clumps on the surface. It is a pliable material, pleated into tubes which, at times, takes on the shape of soft-bodied worms that have become permanently attached to the limestone scaffolding. She imagines these membranous islands as unstable stepping-stones upon which the vengeful and sullen must tread.

Drawing her fingers further along the shallows of the pools, other kinds of soft skins keep time with the slowly rocking thermal currents and seem to beckon her. Some are like strings of beads, while others are spun from gossamer silk threads. Following their traces through the cave, they line the walls in spongy formations, and flourish around damp nooks and crannies.

"These fleshy bacterial mats must be something like the earliest forms of life that I've read about," she says.

"Feed me," Cerebus is pawing at her.

"Oh, *you're* back," says Winnie, scattering handfuls of crumbs as far as she can into the cave and the creature chases off after them again.

"You know, I'm feeling uncomfortably full all of a sudden," she says. "It's like I've just had a big meal, which is very strange, as I've eaten nothing since I've arrived here – unlike *you.*"

She exhales to release the pressure in her chest, but it doesn't move.

"That's so odd," she says. "I've never had asthma."

She tries again but can't force out any breath, so she looks for distractions to take her mind off the uncomfortable tightness building up in her chest.

A host of life forms are flourishing within the pungent atmosphere of the cave – snails, worms, woodlice and shrimp – that are feasting on the bacterial mats. In turn, these are prey for water scorpions, leeches, crayfish, spiders, pseudo scorpions and centipedes. All the creatures are completely transparent and detailed by their innards. None of them possess eyes and all have extremely long feelers and legs.

"I've seen *this* kind of animal before," she says.

"Feed me."

Winnie reaches into her pockets but stops before she throws the crumbs.

"This is your home, isn't it?"

Cerebus shrugs.

"So, where exactly are we?"

The eyeless centipede hesitates.

"I'm not giving you *anything* until you tell me where you've taken me," she insists.

The creature twists around her feet, feeling up her legs and into her pinafore for scraps to eat.

"Shoo! Answer me."

"We're in the Movile Cave," says the worm with a dreadful clatter.

"I need more than that," says Winnie, making sure that the worm can see her playing with crumbs in her pocket.

"We are only a few kilometres inland from the Romanian coast of the Black Sea, in the Constanta County region, but we're *very* far underground."

"It is so alien, here."

"We're a five-million-year-old troglodyte community," says Cerebus.

"You're so odd looking,"

"Speak for yourself! We are proud to be *different*, being entirely transparent."

"Not entirely," says Winnie, as the worm inches closer. "How do you survive?"

"See those clumps of white pond scum? They are our equivalent to plants, here. The lowest order of creatures in the food chain."

"There's no light here, so how do they make their food?"

"They consume poisonous sulphur gases, just as the very first life-forms did."

"So, you're completely self-contained in this underworld?"

"Some are. Others cheat. A few of us are scavengers, feeding on the opportunities that wander into this cave. Fewer than fifty people have been here, you know. That's around the same number of people that have left Earth's orbit to fly around the Moon."

Winnie kicks the worm away from her leg, as it twirls around her in a manner that suggests it's mightily pleased with itself.

"It's the strangest place I've ever seen," she says. "Alf would have loved it. He was always the daring one."

A pale leech wrestles with an earthworm in a macabre dance of death before it drains the worm's body fluids.

Clattering excitedly, Cerebus wraps itself around her leg again. This time, she can't kick it away and it slide up to her chest and touches her face with its feathery antennae.

"Oh, do leave me alone. I detest being groped and slobbered on."

The buttons on Winnie's pinafore seem really tight and she's feeling most uncomfortable with the pressure building up inside her. If she can't exhale, then maybe she can belch.

"Feed me," says Cerebus, moving so close that she can feel its drool slide down her neck.

She pushes the creature's mouthparts firmly away and notices slimy things moving over the rocks.

"I must be hallucinating," she says. "I feel quite peculiar."

The cave walls continue to move. Discrete shapes break away and slither towards her.

"You've led me into a trap, you awful creature," she says.

Several sharp appendages suddenly pin her against the cave wall. Winnie can no longer distinguish between the worm's probing appendages and those of its fellow invertebrates.

"Unhand me now, you devious beasts," she protests, twisting to break free of their blade-like integuments. As their mandibles incise her flesh, she gives one final forceful turn to escape their grip, which releases the pressure inside her chest with an almighty belch that erupts from deep within her abdomen.

Winnie explodes, knocking Cerebus and its companion scavengers right across the cave, back into the recesses from which they came.

With no thought for the logic of the situation, Winnie dives into the grotto and swims underwater for what seems an absolute age. She doesn't check what may be following her and despite travelling for some time, has no desire to draw a breath. Eventually, she moves along with the flow of a warm current, until she reaches a narrow opening of an underwater cavern and wriggles into the space beyond.

Outburst

"I shall retrieve Winnie now, before her soul dissipates."

"It's still not the *right time*, child. Retrieving a recently purged soul endangers the consolidation of her new identity."

"But I can see her so clearly."

"Consider what happens during the putrefaction process. The swelling number of anaerobic bacteria within her corpse produce noxious gasses like methane, hydrogen sulphide and ammonia. These build up inside her abdomen, making her feel uncomfortable. At the point of criticality, when her abdomen bursts open, the blast constitutes the last stand of the microbiota against the encroaching thanatobiome."

"You said that was inevitable."

"Yes, and the point of physical rupture of the corpse marks another transition for Winnie. While the issued blast is not a specific defence mechanism, its force is sufficiently off-putting for scavengers that Winnie's identity is granted temporary reprieve. The newly released thanatobiome, which is sympathetic to her human identity, must now assert itself through its encounters with the more inclusive and expansive necrobiome. However, she remains vulnerable to the inevitable environmental entanglements that follow."

"Then she must be retrieved immediately, Grandmother?"

"No, child. We will imperil the *skeletonisation* process, when her body turns to liquid and is absorbed into the surroundings. The final decomposition event is still a way off yet, but when the process is complete, her body will seem to vanish as a coherent object."

"Then she'll no longer exist."

"She will not have 'gone' anywhere, child. Rather she will disperse into the planetary nutrient cycles."

"That's too risky. We'll retrieve her now, Grandmother."

"No child. She's too fragile. If you intervene at this point, chaos is sure to follow."

Wriggling

The walls of the cave slither under Winne's outspread hand and disperse into nothingness.

"Everything's crawling," she says, "I don't seem to be getting any traction at all."

She turns on to her belly to keep on going.

"Where is that sweet taste coming from?"

As she squeezes through the smallest of gaps, the ground underneath her starts buzzing. The intensity and amplitude of these vibrations grows so strong that she is propelled forward by these oscillations alone.

Transition

"What's that buzzing, Grandmother?"

"Flies, child. They have laid eggs in her flesh and are hatching into maggots that are consuming her soft tissues. Born all at the same time, their individual needs must be synchronously met. Since they prepare for metamorphosis together, they form a throbbing *maggot exodus*."

"What on earth is that?"

"It's the mass migration of larvae, as they move away from the cadaver, each seeking a quiet space in the soil to pupate."

"That's intense?"

"Each larva acts with great effect but lives in a cadaver 'flatland', where no other perspective of space exists. Unable to uncouple their needs from each other, the whole ground comes alive at once. Their increasingly strong vibrations scar the soil with deep yet tiny furrows that radiate from the cadaver like a halo."

"What happens to them?"

"The journey from thanatobiome to necrobiome is forged from many acts of expedience, child. It is not long before the newly hatched flies themselves become prey to other creatures such as skin beetles; mites, ants, wasps and spiders, which re-balance the system towards the next iteration of events."

"Oh, Grandmother, how can Winnie survive such a predatory and unstable environment?"

"Stay vigilant, child. There is much more to come yet."

Soil Body

Crawling through a network of ever-diminishing tunnels, Winnie moves alongside squirming bodies that push their way through the softening soil. A dark, sack-like figure right in front of her abruptly stops. She vaguely recalls a similar situation but can't remember the details.

"What's the problem?" she shouts.

Other formless bodies start pushing her in turn, trying to overtake but they are also gridlocked. Winne follows suit and starts to wriggle sideways into the crowd.

There's more pushing behind her.

"Can we get a move-on, please?" she calls ahead, but is met only by quarrelsome buzzing.

"Perhaps I'm losing my hearing," she says to the murky form to her left. "Or, heaven forbid, maybe I've had another turn."

Sack-like bodies are sliding past her easily now, forming slip-streams that enable her to move. Squeezing past the obstruction, she hears the sound of breaking eggshells and is struck by the unpleasant impression that the stalled body is being actively crushed by others.

"I'm *sure* I've been here before," she says, but decides it best not to ask any awkward questions.

Funnelling alongside the humming crowd, Winnie is quite resigned to ending up goodness-knows-where.

Bacterial Babel

"Why has the humming changed, Grandmother?"

"It's a different language, child."

"Should I know it?"

"It's the language that forms bodies."

"But bodies are made up of structures, not languages."

"No, child. Even in life, the cells in a body stay together by how they communicate with each other."

"What do they say to each other?"

"They speak of identity."

"How do they manage that?"

"Languages demand to be heard, recognised and integrated with each other. Such dialogues are flows of electrons in biochemical exchanges, which take place between every cell, tissue and organ."

"How can they tell what each other is saying, Grandmother?"

"This mutual understanding did not happen suddenly. Electron transfer is life's universal currency, the outcome of billions of years of chemical negotiations, in which human cells are very late members within this community of exchange."

"How does this affect Winnie?"

"She was never a discrete creature, child, but always part of a symbiotic community. In life, her coherent identity is the outcome of many tenuous biological diplomatic processes, which through a diverse range of 'languages' govern the overall behaviour of all complex organisms. In death, however, the voice of the bacterial realm grows louder and more persuasive, dominating these negotiations."

"How do nonhuman languages work, Grandmother?"

"You mean *xenolinguistics*, child."

"What's that?"

"The study of alien languages where *everything that is lively* possesses the power to 'speak'. This includes the decomposition landscape, since it is an unquiet space. The challenge of xenolinguistics is to recognise the various communication techniques that make up the relationships between things, so they can be transposed into our own linguistic preferences."

"But how do things without a mouth, tongue, teeth, palate, chest, lungs, diaphragm and lips actually talk?"

"You're thinking too *literally*, child. Physical *processes* are also languages, since they produce patterns that comprise the *semiosphere*, or realm of meaning. They acquire value as physical languages when they are meaningfully shaped by their context. Bacteria in particular have mastered the art of chemical languages, as they can detect and respond to the accumulation of chemical words, or signal molecules. Making up the basic 'words' of conversation, these substances coordinate important survival functions, including nutrient scavenging, mobility, host immune suppression, and biofilm construction. While many microorganisms have their own specific chemical languages, they can also use the same kinds of substances to communicate with other species. These are not just important to the microbes, but also to people, as their products start to influence or alter our physiology, by changing the way we feel, or think."

"Who, or what, is in control of this process, Grandmother?"

"These are collective decisions. The more recent the transformation from microbiota to thanatobiome to necrobiome, the more seeimngly 'human' the decisions appear to be, as many of these agents hold on to the memories of a particular person as a reference point. As time passes, this memory fades. For Winnie to remain relevant to the expanding necrobiome, she must maintain those conversations that generate her value."

"Then let's retrieve her immediately."

"You lack patience, child. In her present provisional state, she is on the verge of disintegrating entirely."

"Why?"

"Inherent tensions between the ambitions of her thanatobiome and encroaching necrobiome threaten her stability."

"How can I help her?"

"If she is to persist, she must quickly learn new chemical languages – and, if it's any comfort to you – she's getting very good at it."

Heresy

Freed from the stampede, Winnie stands up with some effort, feeling stiff and hot.

The air is scorching and tastes of noxious gases. Puddles of tar ooze from the ground. As she walks, chewing gum-like threads cling to strands of her flesh.

"I'm like a fly in amber," she says.

Her pinafore fibres crackle like popcorn, so Winnie picks up pace.

"If I can reach the surface, everything will be alright. These porous rocks overhead seem to be drawing an air current."

The threads around her ankles are getting thicker, and more numerous.

"The trick is, to keep on moving."

Sticky Stuff

"What's this place, Grandmother?"

"The Door to Hell, child."

"Hell doesn't exist."

"Not in the biblical sense, it's the remains of an old drilling platform shut down in 1971 by Soviet scientists, near the village of Deweze in Turkmenistan. During the day, it is a huge open furnace with leaping flames, and at sunset, an intense beacon said to summon the damned."

"What on earth is she doing *here*?"

"The decomposing dead travel far. Necrobiomes span the world, permeating the ground, air, water and even the most extreme environments. Carried on air currents, they travel as aerosols and through quantum entanglements. Spread across the global highways of terrestrial microbial communities, Winnie's identity is distributed over incredible distances by the flows of the Earth."

"But *how* is she still 'Winnie'?"

"Her evolving thanatobiome adopts a panoramic view of its

emerging identity. The Door to Hell is a bad place for her, though. The incarcerated bodies of the dead creatures in this place, have been transformed by natural and geological forces into *black gold*, or crude oil, which cannot rot, only burn. This is biological heresy."

"Why?"

"The *diagenesis* process rejects decomposition, preserving microbial remains as long-chain hydrocarbons instead, so they cannot re-enter active decomposition networks. Effectively, they are immortal."

"Surely, they deteriorate at some stage, Grandmother?"

"Occasionally, when crude oil spills on to the Earth's surface, a few of these eternal molecules will be oxidised and returned to the living realm. This is hardly a graveyard, though, child. Fossil fuels are organic purgatory."

"Everything's out of place here, Grandmother. Something bad is about to happen."

Darkness

"You're not an innocent," says Winnie. "You're certainly not a geologist. You're up to no good."

"For a *stupid woman*," says Anne, her face darkening, "you make amusingly absurd accusations."

"That poor girl," says Winnie, glaring. "She can't bear you. I know you're doing bad things to her?"

"No good comes of busybodies. They *must be taught a lesson*."

"Exactly what kind of lesson do you have in mind?"

"*That one*," says Anne glaring at the young woman through cats' eyes, "will do *the Devil's work*."

"She will not," says Winnie, "Not on my watch. I *see you now*. You won't make her kill her own baby."

Burning

"There's a terrible stench, Grandmother."

"Where is it coming from, child?"

"It's an incantation, child. Something is being called into existence."

"It's close, Grandmother."

The mortazepam bolus makes it hard to sense what's happening clearly.

"Be careful, child. Things are about to get rough."

Curse

"Take your curse off that poor girl. Right now," says Winnie.

"You haven't a clue what you're dealing with, *busybody*. Keep your nose out of *other people's business*. Be a good *busybody*, now."

"If you don't undo the trouble you cause…"

Anne mutters under her breath, as the young woman, no longer holding her ears, clutches her stomach.

Incineration

Winnie races away from the Door to Hell through its extensive network of plasma tubes.

"This whole place is about to erupt," she says.

A giant worm rears up behind her, flames streaming from its nostrils.

"What the blazes are you?" she yells, heading for a narrow gap between two rocks "and where did you come from?"

Bellowing fire into the tunnel, the rocks are too shallow to protect the lower part of her left leg. As she can't feel it, Winnie keeps on going.

More flames follow her.

"I'll hide in this nook and curl up as small as I can," she says, finding herself at a dead end.

"Stay calm, Winnie," she says from the foetal position as further flames turn the passageway into a furnace. "Worse things will happen if you panic."

A second set of tremors, more plaintive and searching than the first arrive, followed by a whimpering exchange of calls.

Another pyrotechnic volley streams into the passageway. Shrinking back as much as she can, Winnie wonders what Alf might have done under these circumstances.

Then, everything is quiet.

Enough

"Stop!" says Winnie, leaping upon Anne, shaking her viciously.

To her surprise, the tormentor falls suddenly unconscious.

Taken aback at the ease by which she's subdued, Winnie ceases her assault.

All Quiet

"Thank goodness those terrible creatures have gone," says Winnie, "I thought I was done for."

She tries to stand but finds her left leg weakened. When she looks down, there is no flesh but a painless mass that clings to her leg bone. These are not charred remains – but tissues as hard as stone.

"Alf once said that *some things are born of fire,*" she recalls. "He promised to take me to the African savannah one day, where the land is so arid that the plains are wrought with wildfires. Despite this, he said, some creatures found a way to survive. We never made it there, but I read a lot about it."

Resembling a stalactite, her leg is thick at the knee and tapered to the ground.

"Knowing how to survive fire would be very useful right now."

Making her way back to the open tunnels, she traces her stump-leg along the ground, noting how it makes a mark like a stylus.

"Alf said some savannah trees had an insulating corky bark to protect themselves from wildfires, while others moved underground to form forests. Their network of small, thin roots was so widely spread that only the very tips were damaged and could quickly regrow again. Living this way, these invisible forests were almost indestructible and could survive for more than ten thousand years."

Bolstered, she swings her left leg forward, trying to put as much distance between her and the Door to Hell as possible but feels quite off balance.

"Oh goodness my poor leg is like a tree trunk."

Using the sides of the passageway to steady herself, she takes a first step with her right leg, then swings her stone leg forwards pendulum-like. It makes a terrible cracking sound as she walks.

"It's much more of a burden than my old leg, but at least it still works. If I can just figure out how to get myself going, I'll do just fine."

Like so many other things about her present predicament that need sorting out, they can wait until she reaches the surface, where she can safely review everything.

Hatchling

"I thought the worms were a fiction, Grandmother."

"The decomposition landscape is full of incongruities, child, and mythology is integral to its landscape."

"How about *lies*?"

"When ideas, no matter how malevolent, are summoned into existence by repeating them often enough with conviction, they become part of the decomposition landscape."

"How is that possible, Grandmother?"

"The power of suggestion prepares the way for even the most absurd things and anticipates their coming-in-to being. Think of it like preparing a soil for the growth of plants."

"I'm not following, Grandmother."

"The ground where Winnie's corpse lies is now infused with new carbon and sweet volatiles that are seeping into organic layers. This is where the seeds of mythology lie. Conjured into Winnie's imagination by the cat-eyed spirit, a youngling plasma blind worm is now aware of her existence. Disgusted by her rot that contains the molecules of life, it is compelled to erase all traces of her."

All Quiet

Will avoids the glare of oncoming headlight. The rain hasn't backed off and visibility is so poor that he seems caught in an eternal loop of lamp posts, each of which is crying streams of light into the flooded road.

"When will this infernal weather ever stop?" he says, blinking hard to avoid drifting off to sleep.

It's awfully quiet in the back.

Reprise

Swinging along the tunnel with her diamond stump, Winnie senses the heat and all-too-familiar vibrations deep under the ground.

The creatures are back, and they're heading her way.

Trance

Anne's eyes roll upward, exposing their whites. She grabs Winnie with both hands on her chest and hurls her against the back window.

The young woman whimpers pitifully.

"You don't deserve to exist."

Slung like a sack over the seat, Winnie aches as if all her bones are broken. Her left leg feels numb and useless.

"Don't touch her, *you witch*," she says. "You won't get away with this."

Fraud

Brachiating and sprinting with equal ease, Winnie moves undeterred through the tunnel complex with incredible speed and agility over the burning ground. Leaping over fallen rocks, nipping through narrow tunnels and athletically swinging around corners, she uses the traction of her fingertips to gain purchase on all surfaces. The air tastes of brimstone, and a plume of heat screams past her like an angry cry.

The path ahead splits into two.

"Which way?"

She takes the entrance to her left and stops. In front of her is a gaping hole. Noxious organic vapours are rising and condensing on the walls. Sprinting back to the junction, she notices that the number of directions she can take has multiplied since only moments ago.

The heat is upon her again.

"One mistake and I'll be incinerated."

Winnie stops thinking and bolts for her life.

The weight of her pendulum limb launches her over the spongy surface of a tarry lake. On the other side, a large tunnel sprawls out into a network of tubes and she selects a direction without pausing. Another bitumen expanse appears, and another. With every tarry stretch she encounters, she is more decisive, faster and stronger.

A young woman is moving alongside Winne, swinging her left leg like a pendulum. Another athletic figure who is using all her limbs to move through the labyrinth and leaping in a familiar way appears on her right. Synchronously, they clear pitch lakes, yet never speaking or acknowledging each other.

Soon, a whole crowd of runners are continually slipping in and out of view of each other. One falls, another stumbles, a third falters, while some are faced with blind alleys, but each corrects themselves and keeps on running.

The distance between them increases as they continue, and at some point, the surroundings cool sufficiently for moisture to hang in the air.

Wiping the condensation from her brow, Winnie turns to acknowledge her companions but they're nowhere to be seen.

Dispersal

"Where's Winnie now, Grandmother?"

"She has reached the surface of a colossal pitch lake in Trinidad, which reaches down into the Earth's core at the intersection of two tectonic faults around the Caribbean Plate. Sir Walter Raleigh discovered this place in 1595 and used the tar to waterproof his ship. It's so thick you can walk on its surface."

"Can anything survive here?"

"Of course. Bacteria, archaea and strange fungi thrive on a circulation of deep crude oil deposit that is forced up to the surface like ocean currents. The lighter fractions rise first and are simple enough to become food for these extremophiles."

"Can this place support Winnie's necrobiome?"

"Not for long. She is still in grave danger."

"Why?"

"Her carbon molecules are becoming locked in a crystal lattice formation under the extreme pressure in this place, turning her substance to diamond."

"Then she will be indestructible."

"Quite the opposite, child. She will be condemned to eternal purgatory."

"But how?"

"Like crude oil, diamond lacks the capacity for sympathy with life and its conversations through metabolism and therefore separates her organic matter from the decomposition landscape. If she becomes crystalline, she will never be reincarnated."

"Then, I must retrieve her."

"No, child. Too much is at risk. In the blink of an eye, everything that we recognise as Winnie could, all at once, come apart."

Open Door

Winnie rushes Anne with all the strength she's got.

"You will leave her and us alone," she says.

As they collide, Winnie has the presence of mind to open the car door and kicks Anne out of it with the full weight of her dead leg.

"*You can't get rid of me,*" screams Anne. "*I will have my revenge.*"

The door bangs, flaps and slams back shut.

Dark Noise

Sirens screaming, someone vomiting, slurping, shrieking microphone feedback, babies crying, the sound of belching, a railway carriage scraping on a track, snoring, a door's oil-thirsty squeak, someone chewing with an open mouth, fracturing teeth, chimes of an ice-cream van, shifting Styrofoam, someone chewing their fingernails, a humming mains supply, a tortured violin, persistent nose-blowing, a wake-up alarm, a fork scraping on a plate, flatulence, a dental drill, gunshot, a protracted orgasm, nails on slate, more snoring, someone screaming in agony, a dog slobbering on a bone, popular television theme tunes, a stomach growling, defecation, people arguing, a knife scraping against a glass bottle, someone rubbing a balloon, someone explaining the obvious, squealing bicycle brakes, Krakatoa erupting, a toilet flushing, intermittent sniffing, balloons popping, a mother crying.

Seen

"She sees me, Grandmother."

Anne's desperate stare pulls me toward her.

"Whatever you do, child, don't let her back into the car. She'll cling to you so hard, you'll never return."

"I don't know how to stop her, Grandmother."

"Recede, child. Recede."

"I can't. She's deadly."

The green-eyed night closes in on me, as I feel a blush of mortazepam.

Drowning

Who has awakened you
Ancient river of Kent?
Taking all in your wake
You strip lungs of air and
Spew bundles of clothes
Upon your banks as totems
For those that will not return.
This drowning woman turns
To liquid sinking into the
Shadows as if they were leaden
Weights around my ankles
And you my trial by ordeal.
Though you run with intent
For every life you expend
I'll take two, you know.
I order you. Spit me out!
I'm coming back for
You, to do the Devil's
Unfinished work.

Drive On

Will looks around at the terrible noise in the back to see the young woman wide awake and looking anxiously out of the back window.

"Did you lose something?"

"No, no, it's all okay."

"I can stop if you want."

Out on the road a grey figure clad in many smocks stands up. She starts to amble, her cat's eyes glow as she runs towards the boot of the car.

"No! Please, drive on…"

Anne is gaining on them.

"*Your head, your heart, your eyes, your liver, your teeth, your ears, your nerves, your womb, your soul.*"

"Can you go faster?" pleads the young woman, clutching at herself.

"Steady there, missus. *I'm* doing the driving," says Will shaking his head. "Women."

The grey figure is swallowed by a giant wave cast from the wheels of an articulated lorry.

Suddenly free of pain, the young woman turns to see the cat-eyed woman dissolve.

Water

"Did you just intervene, Grandmother?"

"Of course not. Soul catchers never intervene in the affairs of the afterworlds."

"Then did I just lose a soul, Grandmother?"

"No child. A malign spirit was set loose."

Mantlequake

Seismic activity reaches four-point-seven on the Richter scale in Wyoming.

"We cannot account for this unusual activity," says Hank Clinton from the Centre for Economic Geology Research. "There's no tectonic plate movement in this area."

"How do you respond to the observations then, made by experts at Casper College," asks Helen Coleman from the Star Tribune.

"What observations?"

"The tremors originate from the deeper parts of the Earth, around the hotter and more viscous mantle."

"It doesn't make any sense," says Hank, shaking his head. "You media types simply don't want to hear the *facts*."

Treachery

"Alf would have loved travelling around the world like this," says Winne, clambering over a steep ice shelf, using the low-centre-of-gravity swing of her stump leg to speed over the frictionless surface like an ice skater. "He'd never believe what I've been up to."

The steep sides of the cave are sticky where fine ice crystals have coated the rocks and thin threads of meltwater have polished around crevices.

"I wish I had made more effort in building memories together when he was alive and not been such a stick-in-the mud. Although it's not been an easy time of late, I can't say that I've been bored," she says, exhilarated by the speed she's gathering.

"Come to think of it, I have not once thought about what I'm missing on television," she says, realising how odd that might have seemed just a while ago.

As she travels onwards, a faint breeze follows her through the passageways.

"Perhaps I'm close to the way out," she says. "Goodness knows how long things take any more. I'd better pick up the pace and avoid being frozen here."

Reaching an ice cave sculpted into titanic intestinal forms, she feels the vibrations of running water underneath the ground. For the first time since she's been in this predicament, Winnie feels optimistic, even excited. She imagines how the translucent blue walls of the ice caves might be conveying the mood of the sky.

"It's been such a long time since I've seen daylight," she says, projecting a mental image of herself into the realm beyond these spaces, where she's walking out in the open air.

Savouring these splendid moments, she runs her fingertips over a row of spiky icicles. Further over towards the cave wall other ice formation are knobbly like cobblestones and a few of them are sharp, as if they've been ground into blades. Several feel roughly hewn by hand. Exhilarated, she lies down to look up through the roof and imagines she can see the sun.

"How wonderful it's going to feel," she murmurs, "when I break through this ceiling and begin my life anew."

Frozen

"Where's Winnie now, Grandmother?"

"Spores from her thanatobiome have reached the giant Vatnajökull ice cap that forms a natural ceiling over the turbulent volcanic Icelandic landscape, where active fumaroles; geothermal lakes and geysers communicate with the plasma tubes that reach into the Earth's core."

"And her identity?"

"Still evolving."

"Even in such a barren place?"

"It's deceptively fertile terrain, child. Glacial ecosystems are rich in bacteria, algae, diatoms, fungi, and rotifers, which are shaping the constitution of her expanded thanatobiome."

"What is happening?"

"She is in the advanced stages of skeletonisation. Her metabolism is slowing down, allying with ancient chemotrophs whose ancestors became isolated in seawater as the Arctic valleys rose. Obtaining life-promoting carbon dioxide and energy from chemicals released during geothermal activity, their metabolism spans a time frame that is much different from that of warm-blooded creatures. Here, her evolution is reaching a pause."

"Then she must be retrieved instantly, before she disappears."

"Patience, child. The hard work of reconstituting her identity still lies ahead of her."

"Will it *ever* be the *right time*, Grandmother?"

"Haven't you learned, child, there is no easy route to resurrection? Winnie is reaching metabolic equilibrium with the environment, but she is only at the halfway stage to reincarnation, where her physical substance will be assimilated within the bodies of others."

Away

"What just happened back there?" says the young woman, sitting up.

"I'm really not sure," says Winnie, yawning. "Are you okay?"

"I've seldom been better," says the young woman. "You know the best thing?"

Winnie shakes her head.

"The voices have gone. I'm beginning to feel more like *myself*."

"Voices?" says Winnie weakly, and lies back against the car seat. "Do you mind if I lie down here?"

"Not at all," says the young woman, noting how frail the old woman is as she shuts her eyes and how strangely familiar her face seems.

Part III – Purgatory

Compost Elevator

"I will not stand by while you let Winnie fade away."

"You're upset, child. Your recordings are all over the place."

"Don't taint me with your poisons."

"While I admire your passion, child, your impulsiveness is uncalled for. Retrieval of the *right soul* must take place at the *right time*."

"I already *know* what's going to happen. She'll fade under the ice and her thanatobiome's networks will dissipate. Then, she'll be no more."

"She is simply changing, child. We are all shape shifters, both in life and in death."

"How do you mean?"

"From the moment she was born, Winnie's identity has been changing. As a conceptus, she was little more than a speck of jelly. As a foetus, she was a large-headed-jelly-boned body about the size of a small banana. In childhood, she could do roly-polies. As a young woman, she wished to lose her periods, and at the menopause she wanted them back. As an elderly person, she grew stiff and sore, and each day without pain was a blessing. In death, however, her corporeality is infinitely more plastic, since the community of agents that identify as 'Winnie' now work even harder to maintain the identity of her soul."

"Then, if not *right now*, at what point *should* she be ready?"

"Child, you're losing your objectivity."

"Of course, I am."

Mortazepam melts my rising temper.

"Calm yourself, child. There is much cause for comfort. What do you know of the Compost Elevator?"

"The what …? Grandmother. Did you just make that up?"

"Of course not. I'm revealing its name."

"Revealing *what's* name?"

"The Compost Elevator is a natural laboratory formed in a dance between wind, water and fire, shortly after life began. Its deep interconnections draw together the material residues of the earth as loams, clays and peat, embracing the cycles of life and death."

"It's a kind of soil, then?"

"Oh, it's so much more than soil, child. It enfolds life's ephemera into its substance."

"I'm not following you."

"Winnie's reincarnation not only depends on her material traces , but in the choices she makes in her journey through the Compost Elevator."

"It resurrects people?"

"Naturally. How do you think life has subsisted for so long? Winnie's thanatobiome has long been mummified in tarry oils, scattered in aerosols, frozen in diamond, and ingested by invertebrates. Now, she seeks *re-embodiment*."

"Let me retrieve her. I know I can."

"Patience, child. The Compost Elevator does more than nourish the living world, but also regenerates souls. If you are to better understand who, *or what*, 'Winnie' might be, you must accompany her through this place. Even now, fresh sense is being made of her vastly extended necrobiome, as it forges new 'living' relationships with other bodies in its surroundings."

Haunted Spaces

We occupy lonely places with violent
And wicked histories, illuminating the
Impermanence of life and revolving
Hands of time. We have travelled far
Exploring the past, not venturing far,
But deep. Our excavations take place
Without breaking ground, calling out
What happened here. This knowledge
Is active, crossing borders of reality,
Where apparitions and strange events
Bring ominous spaces to life again.

Recovery

The body of a woman in an advanced state of decay is discovered by rescue teams at the site of the collapsed bungalows numbers forty-four, forty-six and forty-eight.

"This is not a complete corpse," says Daisy Chandler, a rookie rescuer. "Perhaps parts of her will end up flushed out into the nearby River Len?"

"Not a chance," says Nora Tell, her superintendent. "Anything we can't retrieve will remain buried under tonnes of sediment in a water-filled void between the sinkhole and the bedrock."

Although the rescuers try hard to keep her remains together, they bring back a set of disarticulated bones, worm-riddled flesh, a generous helping of fragile entrails and a pinafore. These are sent to the coroner for a formal report.

Further into the search area, the bodies of a pair of dog breeders and their dogs are also recovered, in even less coherent a state.

"We think they decided to stay put in their homes, rather than risk their beloved pets being housed in kennels following evacuation by the authorities," says an onlooker.

The gaping hole is filled with twelve truckloads of gravel. With nothing to mark the spot of the disaster, the community soon forget about the strange occurrence.

Autopsy

"Do I *have to* see Winnie in this horrible physical condition, Grandmother?"

"Pay attention, child. The body itself, contains secret information that can be read by ritualistic dissection."

"Gross."

"Nonsense. Such divinations have always been performed by specialists. In ancient times, they were priests, and in modern times specialised doctors decipher the physical traces, which have been written onto the body."

The consultant pathologist lifts her knife to loosen skin, revealing underlying muscle. The remains of Winnie's innards are fused to part of her spine, pelvis and leg bones. Every detail is captured on a personal recording device.

'Last meal; tea and biscuits.

"The heart is flabby, typical of a moderate degree of heart failure.

"Mass 420g. Greasy, pericardium, thin walls of myocardium, all coronary vessels intact, no clots. Pulmonary and aortic valves normal.

"The lungs are full of fluid. Consistent with significant pulmonary congestion.

"There is an osteoporotic spine, which is most pronounced in the cervical and lumbar region.

"Hips are exceedingly arthritic, old right neck of femur fracture. There would have been very little mobility.

"Most of the diaphragm and parts of her the lining around the gut are detached from the body cavity.

On removal and weighing; the diaphragm comes in at 400g, while the omentum reaches 450g.

The liver weighs in at 1,500g while a search for focal lesions conducted in the right, left and middle lobes is negative.

There are no signs of hepatic disease.

It is likely that this female cadaver was dismembered and eviscerated by an explosion. Contributing factors are cardiomyopathy, emphysema. Other findings include moderately severe osteoarthritis."

Burial

Mangravet Avenue and Pheasant Lanes border the limits of Maidstone Cemetery and are much quieter thoroughfares than the Sutton Road. Spanning an area of around twenty hectares, the burial ground has witnessed over thirty thousand internments, whose care and ordering are shaped by strict guidelines . Gates open at ten and are locked at four.

Sunlight caresses the cemetery lawns and daisies smile at the sun, as

Jeremy stands by his mother's open graveside.

When the ceremony's done, a spade full of dirt is placed into Jeremy's hands, which he hurls over Winnie's grave.

"It's a terribly long way down," he says, as crumbs of soil spill over the wooden lid.

As the congregation departs, a small digger drops a loose mound of topsoil over the coffin, piling it high into a little hill. Winnie's necrobiome and organic substances begin to form new relationships with these responsive surroundings. The most ephemeral molecules almost immediately escape the coffin's boundaries and infuse the graveyard earth with their precious chemistry, merging with the metabolic landscapes of many 'others'.

Hitchhikers Eight

"This automatic de-fogging system never works," says Will, blasting the power to full. "I'll just have to do things the old way."

The visibility is terrible.

He wipes the rear-view mirror with his sleeve, but it remains misted. Then, he opens and shuts the window several times.

"At least *that* button works," he says.

Through liquid streaks he glances back at the young woman.

She's awake, her clothes are drying and she's significantly calmer. Catching his gaze, she smiles briefly and presses her nose against the window without leaving a breath mark.

"At least the air conditioning is working in the back," he says, "I can turn it down if you like."

She does not reply.

A lorry turns left just ahead of them, casting a wave of rainwater across the windscreen. Nothing seems to stop the freight traffic on this road.

"I'm sure I passed the Old Palace ages ago," he says, "there it is again on the left."

More water washes over the vehicle.

"Isn't that the Old Palace again?"

He wipes a small hole in the windscreen fog with his sleeve.

"Oh, I don't know. Frankly this smear of buildings could be anything."

He checks the rear-view mirror again.

"What did you say your name was, miss?"

Part IV: Resurrection

Water Table

Winnie wakes to the sound of running water.

"It seems the ice has melted," she says.

Around her, limestone fingers dribble into overflowing pools.

"Maybe, if I follow this water to its end, it will show me the way out *this place*."

Something flutters above her.

"Who on *earth* might you be," she says. "A bat, perhaps. Are you hurt?"

She stops to follow the creature, but it stops moving exactly when she does.

"Show yourself," says Winnie, feeling emboldened by its timidity.

Still, it refuses to declare itself.

"I know what you are. You're a *mechanical moth*."

Rope-like tributaries thicken the girth of the twisting stream, which steadily picks up speed. She continues walking, listening to the sounds within the network of caves.

Something 'else' seems to have joined her. Two wary pinpoints glitter now and again, maintaining a wary distance.

After a while, they start purring.

"Here, kitty," calls Winnie reassuringly, but nothing wants to approach.

"How unfriendly this place is," she says, noting how uneven the terrain has become. The path loses its continuity and she has to hop between islands to follow the direction of the water.

"Which one of these streams shall I pursue?" she says.

A coarse vibration is coming from the nearest of the tunnels, so she walks towards it.

"Perhaps it's a pig."

Sharp nails scramble alongside her from rock to rock as the rasping animal rambles alongside her with a rolling gait.

"Good boy," she says. "I mean no affront, but I won't call you hither."

The underground passages are splitting up again, so she stops to take her bearings with the grunting, pinpoint flickers and fluttering in tow.

"The water's so turbulent, it's impossible to tell its direction of flow."

She reaches into her pinafore pockets, looking for something that might float on the water, but finds they're empty.

"I'm sure I didn't use up all those crumbs," she says.

She pauses, feeling an extremely weak presence close by.

A boy with the body of a man, or a man with a child's countenance, steps out from a cleft in the tunnel and stares at her.

"Hello, I'm Winnie," she says and stretches out her arm to shake hands.

He ignores the gesture.

"I'm looking for the way out," she says.

The man-boy shifts from one foot to the other.

"Are you looking for the way out too?"

Perhaps he can't understand her very well.

"We're just trying to find the way out down this tunnel," she says. "You're welcome to join us."

Coils of water leap up at them, as they pick their way together over the broken ground.

"Is that your dog?" he says, after a while.

Warily, the black and white bull terrier approaches.

"He's looking for the way out too," says Winnie.

"Looks like a fighter," says the man-boy. "What's his name?"

"I don't think he has one," she says.

The man-boy pauses for a while, then brightens.

"Jim. Come here boy!"

The dog, wobbles excitedly around in circles.

"Poor thing, its back legs appear to be dragging a little," says Winnie.

"Come here, Jim," says the man-boy. "Over here."

It tries to jump up at him, lopsided, wagging its tail but cannot clear the ground.

"Why do you call him Jim?"

"Same name as my brother."

Winnie nods.

"Did you lose contact?"

The man-boy continues to fuss the dog.

"Over here, Jim. No, *here*, you, dumb animal," he says, pushing the dog roughly away from him.

Quarrelling male voices resonate from the cave complex.

"We have company," she says and stands up briskly, ready to run.

"Good day, madam. Good day, all. Henry Bollen, at your service," says a brightly uniformed man, rocking back on one heel and sweeping a low bow before her.

Winnie is taken aback by the stranger's courteous manner.

"Good day, sir," she says, with a reciprocal display of etiquette. "You may call me Winifred."

To her own surprise, she bobs a curtsey.

While her full name seems overly formal, remembering her manners seems quite fitting for this strange occasion.

"Is that rascal harassing you, Miss Winifred?" asks Henry's tall companion. "Thomas Merton, your servant."

He gives the man-boy a stern look while he too, bows graciously low.

"Well, no. He's…" She tugs on the boy's sleeve, who is rather taken aback by her vote of confidence.

"John, sir." He looks meekly at his feet, pushing the dog, who doesn't seem to be able to believe that it's getting so much attention. Even if it's inappropriately rough, now and again.

"Madam, may we accompany you?"

"I'm looking for the way out," says Winnie. "Perhaps we should travel together. I've been following the flow of the water, but I'm wondering whether I'm on the right track."

"Then, Miss Winifred, you have come across the right gentlemen to escort you," says Henry. "We are looking to rejoin our troops at the Battle of Maidstone."

Winnie wants to ask if that particular battle was a very long time ago but waits for things to become clearer.

"As professional soldiers, it's our duty to make sure no harm comes to a lady as graceful as you," adds Thomas.

"Oh goodness, I'm nothing special," says Winnie. "Just a silly old woman but thank you all the same."

Thomas and Henry look at each other and then laugh aloud for quite a while.

"If you insist, madam," says Thomas.

They carry on together following the stream until they reach a stony shelf meandering around a series of islands.

"The water is picking up speed," says Winnie and runs ahead to see if there are any signs of an exit.

The two quickly men catch her up.

"Dear Winifred," says Henry. "I wonder if you can help us."

"Of course," she says.

"My colleague and I have a difference of perspective," says Henry. "Thomas is from the New Model Army and I am the servant of our good King Charles. In this way, we are sworn mortal enemies."

"Gentlemen, please stop your dispute at once!" says Winnie. "There is no contradiction here. England has both queen and parliament. They work together to represent our people."

The two men stare at each other in disbelief. Then, they fall around laughing again.

After a dreadfully long time, Thomas and Henry recover their senses, setting off along the side of the limestone walkways together their differences apparently, reconciled.

Only a few minutes later, Thomas and Henry begin laughing again.

"Gentlemen, *please*," urges Winnie. "We need to focus if we're going to complete this mission together."

Momentarily reprimanded, the soldiers lead the merry band of unlikely travellers on its way – a 'mechanical moth', an invisible cat, a wobbly dog, a sullen man-boy and a young woman, who doesn't yet realise that she's no longer old.

Changing

"Grandmother, there are so many souls now, it's difficult to tell them apart."

"I warned this would be challenging, child."

"Who are they?"

"They are echoes, eddies and shades of past beings. These phantoms have suffered trauma and loss and are in search of new forms of peace within the Compost Elevator."

"Why are they so drawn to Winnie?"

"She's such a strong soul that she naturally attracts such negotiations. Composted bodies are not discrete objects. By definition their boundaries are open to new influences and may be distributed across vast areas and time spans. Winnie's scattered remains intersect with traces of these travellers and each are in search of reincarnation. They view her as a way back to the living realm."

"Where do they come from?"

"They are re-distillations of previous identities that have already been materially dissipated through various migrations of their thanatobiome, necrobiomes and vagrant spirits. While the residues of these shades did not exist in the same time and space as Winnie when she was living, they are brought together within the Compost Elevator. Here, carbon atoms from the bodies of soldiers, berries eaten by the 'mechanical moth', vermin caught by the cat, and timbers of the sad home of the shifty young man, are entangled. Soon, they will be reanimated via new material expressions."

"How is that possible? Winnie's buried in a wooden box under the ground."

"A graveyard plot is a symbolic resting place, child. It does not prevent rotting bodies from leaking volatile gases and aerosols into the ground, water and air. Parts of Winnie that were not recovered from the sink hole are now dissipated through the Kent aquifer, and far beyond that still."

"These travellers are getting in the way of the retrieval process, Grandmother."

"Don't be petulant, child. You must wait for the *right time*."

"When is it *ever* the *right time* to retrieve her, Grandmother? You yourself have said she's in grave peril."

"Pay close attention, child. These shades are not only making physical connections with Winnie, but they are also altering her fate and helping her achieve reincarnation."

"Then, I must retrieve her before she irreversibly changes."

"No, child. You will needlessly put her entire being at risk. To successfully recognise the *right time* and *right soul*, you must first understand how the Compost Elevator works."

Ode to Compost

Children and animals enjoy their friendship
With dirt, and might even be expected to perish
From their indulgence of contaminated matter
But healthy soil matrixes ensure they survive.
While fertile soils are full of death and decay,
They're much richer in life. Nurturing communities
Of worms, fungi, microbes, nematodes, diatoms,
Centipedes, beetles, spiders, ants and woodlice,
Nothing dead in the soil stays that way for long:
Even humans make room for other organisms.
In death, we're processed, cleansed and incubated
In our final resting place, turning into compost,
Which invests its dark energy through countless
Acts of metabolic transformation. Filtering our
Fetor, the ground draws in air as exquisite winds
That enable us to breathe anew. In the earth
Our rotting remains are animated to become
Vibrant expressions of matter that collectively,
Compose the webs of life within the ecosphere.

Battle of Maidstone

"It's daytime, but it's dark, Grandmother."

"Something is interfering with your life-force, child. Stay focussed."

"I'm passing a narrow bridge."

"I see Thomas."

"Keep talking. I will reconfigure the apparatus and retrieve you if necessary."

"He is walking, no, *marching*, with General Fairfax's New Model Army, from East Farleigh towards Maidstone."

"Concentrate, child. Your biometrics are erratic."

"He's fighting hard for every inch against the thousand strong Royalists, but is forced into retreat at Gabriel's Hill."

"Keep at a distance, child."

"There's a terrible thunderstorm. Henry's here, vigorously defending the Royalist stronghold in the churchyard. Oh no! He is badly wounded."

"Stay away from the shades, child, you cannot save anyone."

"Thomas is gravely ill. The relentless rainfall and tough conditions are taking their toll."

"These phantoms will weaken your own soul unless you return them to the Compost Elevator."

"But how, Grandmother?"

"Link me in to the memory of their original death, child. Then, I can re-set the apparatus"

"Quickly, Grandmother! They are in the chapel grounds, side by side. Each struggles with their own malady but perish together with barely a whimper."

Something sears through my veins.

"Your biometrics are picking up again, child."

I want to throw up, but instead, swallow a deep bitterness welling up from the pit of my stomach.

"Everything's dark, Grandmother. Will they find peace?"

"There's no peace with a *country* at odds with its identity, child."

Echoes

"This rock formation is a chalk aquifer," says Winnie, running her fingertips over its porous surface. "We're likely to be moving along a water table."

"What kind of a *table?*" says Thomas.

"Not furniture," says Winnie.

"Then why say it, then?" says Thomas.

"It's a scientific term that describes where the ground has no spare capacity to soak up rainfall. This means water pools, form a flat surface here, *a kind of table*, on top of the clay beneath it."

"Makes no sense to me," says Thomas.

"Well, if I'm right and we stay on this pathway, then we'll find a way out through a spring," says Winnie.

"Just get me out of here," says Thomas.

Empathy Storm

Rehearsing for our reincarnation
And how we possibly will, one day,
Walk round in someone else's skin
Requires empathy. Collectively we
Use our mental agility to conjure
Experiences beyond our memories
In search of other languages that
Enrich our souls. To empathetically
Re-enter the world, we reorganise
Our senses, our understanding, our
Desires: the nature of our existence.

Envisaging ourselves as unfamiliar
Beings: monsters whose very nature
Causes us to struggle. This 'game' of
Imagination fuels our empathy and
Makes us cry, but these games don't
Help us care for 'others'. Knowing
Starved of change isn't empathy.
Emotion without aid isn't empathy.
No matter how many sad games we
Play, or tragic encounters we simulate:
if we are to be re-born, then we must
Establish empathy with others, first
Changing ourselves from within.

Bedrock

"There's no sign of your spring yet, woman," says Thomas.

"Let's spread out," says Winnie. "I'll take this narrow opening to the right, and report right back."

"Then I must accompany you," insists Henry.

"I'll be just fine by myself," she says.

"It's a dangerous place to get lost," says Thomas.

"I appreciate your concern but I do not need an escort," says Winnie. "Why don't each of you take those larger passageways instead. We'll cover more ground that way. We can meet back here shortly to share what we've found."

"What if we lose you?" asks Henry.

"I won't go too far, and nor will you. John can wait with the others."

The soldiers glance at each other and shrug, separating to explore the larger openings.

"You'll wait here for us, John." says Winnie.

The man-boy plays with Jim, refusing to acknowledge her.

Striding across a number of fractured steppingstones Winnie slips through the gap in the tunnel and into a series of restricted passageways, where the water has pooled to the point of stagnation.

"There are no tell-tale sounds of an exit here," she mutters.

Something flickers past her face.

"Don't leave me alone in the dark," chirrups the mechanical moth.

Its voice is remarkably clear and powerful.

"Of course not," says Winnie. "Stay close to me."

It flutters so close to her face that Winnie recognises the creature as a tiny wren.

Returning to the meeting point together, the wren stays close to Winnie, as on arrival, mayhem is evidently afoot.

John and Jim are in a standoff with the cat, which has stretched into a grey arch, hissing and spitting at them from the shadows. For the first time, Winnie notices that between its fiery yellow eyes is a gaping hole.

"What on earth is going on?" says Winnie.

"That devil lashed out at Jim," claims John.

"I did not," hisses the cat. "That brute invaded my space."

"Oh, for goodness sake! There's plenty of room down here. Why don't you just move to another place to play, John?"

"We were here first."

"You *invaded* my dry spot."

"What's your story, Jim?" says Winnie.

"It's just a cat," says the dog.

"Why don't you both wait over there until Henry and Thomas return," says Winnie, gesturing towards a dry and generous shelf at some distance from the cat, "there's more room for you both."

"Whatever.," says the man-boy, passing defiantly close to Winnie.

Soon, John and Jim strike up a game of "water fetch". John throws a stick into the stream for the dog to retrieve but every time he brings it back, he hurls it into the water again.

The cat grins at the action from its dog-free space.

Without enough intelligence or coordination to always succeed in bringing back the stick, Jim returns for directions. Instead of helping the dog, John kicks it back into the water until, half-drowned, and by sheer luck, Jim find the stick.

Concerned about how tired and disoriented the dog is getting, Winnie raises her hand to put a stop to the game, just as Thomas returns.

"Madam, there are no signs of flow in that cave," he says.

Henry arrives a few moments later.

"This way," he says.

The motley travellers pick their way over treacherous limestone plates, happily unhappy in each other's company, as none would consider navigating this treacherous place on their own.

Unruly

"A terrible storm is brewing, Grandmother."

"You're getting too close to the shades, child, and risk becoming a permanent part of the decomposition landscape. If this happens, then I cannot bring you back."

"But this tempest threatens the integrity of the wren's spirit."

"The bird has a *soul*, child. *Every* living thing has a soul. Bacteria have souls. Birds, cats, dogs and centipedes have souls, and each has a unique journey towards reincarnation, but you must be less involved with these shades. They are exploiting your empathy. Concentrate on the details of the decomposition landscape."

"I'm following the storm's raw violence. Nothing is safe. Hops, apples, cobnuts and corn are destroyed across twenty-four parishes stretching from Tunbridge Wells to Sheerness. Oak, beech, sycamore, chestnut, ash and aspen trees are stripped of nearly all their leaves. It's killing every living thing in its path from foxes, hares, badgers, otters and stoats, to pheasants and partridges. Houses are blown down and massive hailstones shatter the lead-framed windows along the whole of Maidstone high street. Some of these measure twenty-five centimetres in diameter."

"Don't get too close to the bird. I'm going to re-set your baseline biometrics.."

"The poor thing is afraid. It's trying to protect its young family, but as it tucks them in safely, the air is sucked out of its chest."

"Be comforted, child. After these wicked winds die down, the whole community comes back together. Those who lost their livelihoods are overwhelmed by the generosity of commoners, gentlefolk and creatures alike that rally around survivors. With their remarkably high egg productivity, within only a few years, the entire wren population is fully recovered."

"Then, souls can be *happy* in the *ever after*?"

"Of course, child, but the Compost Elevator does not actively seek happy endings."

"What do you mean by that, Grandmother?"

"While it draws bodies and souls together that are in search of new forms of peace, it cannot erase the fundamental injustices that occur in nature. Nor does it alleviate primal tensions, such as that between dog, cat and bird."

"But we're perfectly poised to intervene, Grandmother."

"That's just not the way it works, child."

"But, why?"

" At last! Your biometrics are back on track."

Compressed

It's crowded here.
We make the most of this space
Aligning ourselves in repeating
Periodic patterns and
Three-dimensional lattices
But it's not enough.

Homogeneity stifles our character,
So we need another
Arrangement with more dimensions,
Capable of filling
All available space
Without replication.

Trapping photons in our lattices,
We absorb and reflect light
That moves around us
But does not propagate
Through us.
With this key to manipulating
The solid universe,
We can make it disappear.

Weathering Rock

"These limestone shelves are increasingly fragile," says Winnie. "This is much softer sedimentary rock called 'greensand'."

As her companions are sullen, she whistles a rather old and simple tune called the 'Whistle Song', which eerily resonates within the cave system.

The creatures stop momentarily, pricking up their ears at the strange melody.

"Pray do not do that, madam," snaps Henry.

"Why ever not?"

Thomas is more direct.

"Only cunning women whistle."

"Cunning?"

"Are you are casting a spell on us, wench?" says Thomas, striding towards her, his arm accusatively outstretched.

"I am not," says Winnie.

"Yet you are accompanied by familiars – the dog, the cat, the bird," says Thomas. He looks suspiciously at the teenager. "That *fellow* you're with. *He's not quite right at all.*"

John's face lengthens, while Jim paws at his leg for attention.

Thomas stares Winnie down.

"Do you deny that the world is ordered by hidden forces that can be controlled or influenced by the use of rituals and magical ceremonies?"

"Well, sir." Winnie remembers her graces, particularly in the face of aggression. She read that it could be disarming. "I really don't know what you mean?"

"Are you a concubine of Satan? Confess woman. Or I swear I shall force it out of you," he thunders.

"*Well, I never,*" says Winnie.

Thomas grabs her roughly by the arm.

"You will confess!"

"Unhand me now, sir. You are most inappropriate."

Stirred by the possibility of dispute with his companion, and a growing sense of heavy-handedness in the matter, Henry takes a contrary view of the matter.

"Step down, sir. You misjudge the good woman."

"Misjudge? She was summoning the winds."

"Sir, put away your ire, it is misplaced?"

Thomas lets go of Winnie's arm.

They fall gravely silent. Even Jim's grunting quells.

"But you *heard* the wench," says Thomas after a while.

"Sir, I will not be referred to as wench, whore, strumpet or any other term that your tongue would sleight me with. I have done you no harm and mean neither of you ill will."

She immediately lowers her voice and calms her tone.

"I believe we are in the midst of a misunderstanding."

She steps quickly back and raises her chin in a dignified manner.

Surprised by her vigour and clarity of argument, Thomas relents. After all, she's strikingly handsome and it would be a pity to condemn her.

"Aye, it is true that the elements have not been summoned. But pray, Henry. How do *you* account for this eternal purgatory that so affronts us? Are we not thwarted here in our very duty of battle?"

"'Tis true, brother," admits Henry, "but were we not in this place a long time before we came across this dear lady, who has provided such charming company amongst the gloom. Come now. I think the whistling was a bird."

The wren chirps shockingly loudly on cue. It sounds nothing like the *Whistle Song* but at least, it gets the rhythm right.

"It was the bird," asserts Winnie. Knowing it's a *white lie* and feeling most uncomfortable at this endorsement.

"I heard her whistle." Says John.

Before Winnie can gather her wits, Henry strikes John sharply across the face with his glove.

"You speak out of turn, rascal. Know your place. You will not utter another word until you are spoken to."

Although she wants to thank Henry for his words, which ring sharply in her thoughts, she says nothing, since *that* should be the final pronouncement on this matter.

The wren chirrups something that mimics the *Whistle Song* a few more times, before vanishing.

The subdued band of travellers continue on their way; their thoughts are like stones and full of misgivings.

Hidden

"What a changeable place this is, Grandmother."

"Be careful, child, the Compost Elevator is capable of many acts of concealment and revelation. Some of these have long been regarded as devious acts, or *occult* forces. Seemingly, they subvert the course of natural events, which may render the ordinary, extraordinary."

"How so?"

"Take, for example, the mineral deposits that surround these unquiet travellers, which conceal many transformations. The calcium-rich sandstone, which forms the Greensand hills in the Weald also contains a subset of earths like the dark blue-grey sandy mudstones of the Atherfield Clay formation. The whole place is a witches' brew of rubblestone and sands of varying grain size, which are mixed with siltstone, mudstones and limestone in the most extraordinary manner."

"It sounds remarkably commonplace, Grandmother."

"That's part of the deception. These earths forge a unique ecosystem ranging from the rich terrains that promote chestnut, hazel and oak forest, to poorer quality soils that support the growth of Scots pine and birch copses. Such soils have long been attributed with a deep knowledge and vigour for life. You might prefer to think of them as site-specific forms of *magic*."

"An environment isn't magic, Grandmother. It's a rational organisation of the living world that is particular to a specific place. Such life forms are inevitable here."

"Then you mistake the extraordinary for ordinary, child. Why do you think that such bodies exist nowhere else in the cosmos?"

Proud

"Why don't we each tell a story to pass the time?" suggests Winne.

Henry immediately steps up to the challenge.

"On New Year's Eve, a hundred and fifty knights sit at King Arthur's round table. Each upholds the ideals of chivalry and the rule of order across the land," he begins. "Suddenly, a Green Knight interrupts the festivities and challenges them all to a game.

"I will endure a strike to the neck from the bravest of you," says the Green Knight, "if, a year and a day from now, that same knight submits to a blow from my own sword in return."

Silence spreads across the hall, as the invitation is to submit to death.

"Is this the court for its courage renowned?" scoffs the knight.

The king rises to his feet, but before he can make his oath, Sir Gawain takes Arthur's place.

"Finally, a man worthy of this court's reputation," says the Green Knight. "You may now take your blow, sir."

The knight lowers his head and exposes his neck. Gawain strikes his mark true with an axe and the knight's head rolls across the floor. Then, to the court's surprise, the decapitated body stands up, picks up its severed head. Turning to Gawain, the Green Knight reminds him of his pledge.

True as his word, as a year and a day approaches, Gawain seeks out the Green Chapel where he is to meet the knight at the appointed time. Chancing upon the Castle Hautdeser, he is welcomed by Lord Bertilak.

"I will be your host while you await your meeting with this Green Knight," says Lord Bertilak, "on the condition that we will both share everything we receive during your stay."

Taking a liking to Gawain, the lady of the household gives Gawain kisses on the first two days. This, the stalwart knight returns to his host. However, on the third day she offers him a girdle as protection from the Green Knight. Fearing for his life, he keeps this secret from his host.

The next day, Gawain meets the Green Knight and submits to his blow but is only grazed by the axe as he is protected by the girdle. Revealing his true identity as Bertilak, the Green Knight tells Gawain he has been cursed by the enchantress Morgan LeFay. Having broken his oath, Gawain asks for his forgiveness, but is eternally humbled by shame for his fallibility and weakness.

Returning to court with a hero's welcome, Gawain pledges himself anew to both God and king. Upholding the virtues of knighthood with renewed vigour, he offers a model of friendship, generosity, chastity, courtesy, and piety that brings fresh justice and truth to the land."

"That's a terribly sad story," says Winnie.

"It's what heroes do," replies Henry. "They give things up for others."

"Poor Gawain is tortured by his own human weakness," says Winnie, "rather than celebrating the goodness he brings to the world."

"You have it all wrong, good woman," says Henry. "The story is not about a man at all, but a parable that asks whether heavenly virtue can ever exist within a morally bankrupt world."

"If the country's reputation was put into the hands of the people, rather than a treasonous king and his privileged 'foreign' men," says Thomas, "then that story would have a different ending."

"God appoints the king, sir," retorts Henry. "Are you questioning the judgement of God?"

"Ah, sir," replies Thomas, "My quarrel is not with the Lord, nor with the noble knight, but with the malign temptations of women. No good ever comes of that." He looks purposefully at Winnie. "The fair sex brings their own kind of trouble."

"But the Lady Bertilak and the knight did nothing wrong."

Winnie quickly bites her lip, to prevent herself saying the *wrong* thing.

"She is a temptress, just like the witch Morgan LeFay," says Thomas. "Even when such wenches pledge to serve the people, they bring nothing but trouble."

"Do tell us more," says Henry. "It's your turn to share a story now."

"At the time of the Hundred Years War, when northern France still belonged to England," says Thomas, "Joan, *The Maid of Orléans*, was born to poor tenant farmers. Charged with caring for the family's animals, she was troubled by mystical visions that persuaded her to exchange her domestic duties for a pious life. Convincing the local community she was speaking directly with God, she gained support and set out to support the expulsion of the English from France and install Charles VII as the rightful king.

Against his better judgement, Robert de Baudricourt gave the wench a horse and an escort of several soldiers. Promptly adopting male attire, she cropped her hair before making her way to Chinon, the site of Charles's court. Deeply suspicious of this peasant girl who professed she could save France, the nobleman ordered her to be examined by prominent theologians, and found her to be properly pious, chaste and humble, so Joan was allowed to accompany the army to an English siege at Orléans, where French troops took control of the English fortifications. Although wounded during the battle, she returned to rally a final assault and victory, filling the hearts of the troops with courage. Charles was then crowned at Reims, with the young woman visibly at his side.

The battle for sovereignty, however, was not yet won.

During a fresh battle at Compiègne, the woman was thrown off her horse and taken captive by the Duke of Burgundy's men, who were allies of the English. Symbolising France's courage, English church officials used her status to demoralise the resistance by charging her with the sins of witchcraft, heresy and *dressing like a man*. Taken to Rouen marketplace, she was burned at the stake before a crowd of 10,000 people, where only her heart survived the fire. The rest of her ashes were scattered in the Seine."

"It is indeed strange, sir, that you esteem such an enemy of England," says Henry. "Surely that's the tale of a traitor."

"The point I am making, sir, is that no man, not even a king, should endorse the actions of witches, regardless of how sincere, or adept, their protestations may be."

"That is what you *say*, sir," says Henry, "But I detect an air of *admiration* for fearless Joan."

"Sir, you mistake my manner for the satisfaction I take, regarding her unnatural abilities, *in the justice that was finally done.*"

The travellers return to silence brought by these incendiary tales and Winnie makes no further attempts to invite conversation.

Reaching another decision point in their journey, the soldiers volunteer to explore the pathways ahead and return.

For the first time since her betrayal, Winnie is alone with John.

"So, what's your story?" She asks.

John stares vacantly through her.

"Don't pretend you don't know what I'm talking about. Why did you try to make trouble for me?"

The man-boy remains silent.

"I'm going to find out what you're hiding, and when those soldiers know about it, you'll be making your explanations to them, not me."

She stands resolutely before him.

"I wanted to see what they'd do to you," he finally says.

"I'll remind you that we're all in a very difficult situation and if we don't work as a team and figure out our difficulties and disagreements, then none of us will ever make it out of this purgatory."

John shrugs and goes off to play with Jim.

"Here, Jim. Fetch. That's it, fetch the stick."

Thomas returns with news about a convincing flow in the tunnel to the left of the cave complex and they all wait quietly for Henry to return and report his findings.

John distractedly plays with the dog.

In the dreadful silence that ensues, Winnie wishes she had never learned to whistle.

Henry returns from the endless cave complex with a spring in his stride and a broad smile on his face.

"I have good news," he says. "Did you miss me?"

They all did.

Sub Soil

"Why is there so much friction between Winnie and her companions, Grandmother?"

"None of them can exist in limbo indefinitely, so if their souls are to be reincarnated, then radical changes in the order of things must lie ahead. The Compost Elevator is exploiting these tensions to provoke tipping points in their relationships. At the same time it is bringing them into proximity with the organic realm through its mixology of potions, memories, desires, freedoms and promises."

"How does is such far-reaching change possible?"

"The pathway to reincarnation takes place in stages within various soil *horizons*. Each zone has a particular character that enables the water, air, minerals, myths, memories, quantum eddies, mutable agents and wandering spirits to come together and produce their effects."

"Like an industrial assembly line?"

"It's much more inventive. Take for example the A-horizon, which is the most resourceful soil layer. Here, dead bodies initially fall alongside litter, humus and top mineral soil. Through the Compost Elevator, this layer becomes a vigorous site of mixing, vanishing and re-appearing, where a broad spectrum of metabolic activity transforms organic substances into easily dissolved compounds that leach into the lower layers. Collisions between agents here can result in radical reorganizations of necrobiotic and existential identity."

"So, it *shapes* character?"

"Not exactly, but the B-horizon is an alchemical realm of subtle transformations and personality development. This mineral subsurface is a zone of accumulation, which receives materials washed out of the A-horizon such as clay, soluble salts, souls, mythological fragments and iron, where organic complexes are shaped by geostories, ghosts and dreams."

"How long does this take?"

"Sometimes things happen quickly in a matter of days but at the C-horizon, the reincarnation process slows right down to the scale of a lifetime. The matrix here is much less flexible and relationships between agents mature more slowly. Every horizon has its own rhythm. Deep down in the R-horizons, which are made of stable material such as sandstone, limestone or clay, regenerating bodies are largely inert. Since they are unchanging, this place is a prelude to eternal rest, or fossilisation."

"How do reincarnating souls acquire character?"

"Within zones of great learning at the O-horizons, where carbon-rich plant litter and vagrant desires are transformed into receptive matter through the bodies of soil bacteria. Frequently waterlogged, these black water-retaining litter zones learn how to vie with each other for their ongoing persistence. Since there is not enough oxygen to fully decompose organic matter, partial beings passing into this layer must invent anaerobic processes – and it smells like Hell."

"That's a joyless process."

"Not at all. The Compost Elevator is highly emotionally charged. Rapture resides in the flamboyant space of the fibric soils within the L-Horizon, while the hemic soils of the F-Horizon that are characterized by intermediate forms of decomposed organic matter, are diligent spaces. There are also sad zones that can be found within the highly decomposed sapric soil layers, or H-horizons, which are rich in liquefied organic matter."

"How do souls know where to go in this crazy matrix, Grandmother."

"They don't, child. The Compost Elevator provides no guidance, since it has no formal moral code. Instead, it enables competing interests to play themselves out. Like soul catchers, it retains a neutral stance and cannot be accountable for individual choices. Needless to say, not every decision that takes place is desirable, nor upholds the unbroken legacy of life."

"Why doesn't it intervene, Grandmother? The Compost Elevator is perfectly placed to decide what is right and wrong."

"Not every soul is destined for reincarnation. Some are trapped within destructive cycles of re-embodying, which leads them nowhere and in some cases, this may actually be the best place for them."

Wrathful

The travellers follow the swiftly running stream, which promises the quickest way out,

Although Winnie is sympathetic towards Jim and its piggish manner, John increasingly troubles her. While she wants to attribute his apparent lack of empathy with poor education, or terrible upbringing, his blank stare, lack of concern for others, unwillingness to talk with anyone and his preferential distancing from everyone, suggests he has little care for his companions.

"Don't you dare get comfortable thinking that way, Winnie," she mumbles, hoping this will stop the feelings from amplifying. "Bad thoughts only bring unhappiness. He's just a young man with much to learn."

Encouragingly, she has managed to strike an extremely uneasy peace with Thomas, who reserves his hostility providing she adopts a deferential manner. While this is an unsatisfactory state of affairs, she's making the best of things.

"Keep your head, Winnie. We'll be out of here soon enough."

Sharing his observations of the labyrinthine caves, Henry keeps everyone's spirits up and even seems to be enjoying himself.

"There goes a magnificent eel," he says, as if seeing one for the first time.

It takes a little time for the cat to stop staring at the monster.

"Here is a beautifully formed finger of rock, with curves like a woman," continues Henry, running his fingers over its silky surface.

Further along he notes, "This dripping is the sound of a drum," which unconsciously, prompts them all to march in time with its beat.

The wren flutters into the tractionless space, as if surveying a prospective home.

"There are times when being in this gloomy predicament isn't so bad at all," says Winnie, noting surface eddies that suggest the river is steadily picking up speed.

"Over here," shouts Henry from within a low-lying cloud of thick water vapour. "The rock formation is changing. I think we've reached a new phase in our journey."

One by one they follow his voice into the fog.

"I do *hope* so," says Winnie.

Momentarily, Henry stops to make sure everyone is keeping up. As Winnie bumps into him, she squeezes his hand for reassurance.

Unobserved by the others, they walk quietly together for a while with knotted fingers, until the saturated air abates and the unpleasant atmosphere they have acclimatised to, returns.

Tears

"This decomposition landscape is exhausting, Grandmother."

"The Compost Elevator materialises the afterworlds, so the desires and emotions of the travellers become increasingly real."

"How do you mean?"

"Winnie's thoughts are creating atmospheric impurities. Carried on flimsy gases, they form self-replenishing circulations of water vapour like mist, cloud and fog – which reduce visibility."

"Is she hiding something, Grandmother?"

"Of course, child. These clouds of water vapour not only produce events but also conceal them. The salty droplets formed by heated and chilled emotional fields, condense within her lacrimal glands. Squeezed through their delivery ducts, they sting her cheeks and *hurt like Hell.*"

"She's crying, Grandmother."

"Tears can repress, or conceal, vulnerabilities. Crying is also a transformative experience, which releases stress and stirs empathy in others."

"I feel sorry for her."

"Don't get too attached to the shades. These clouds are here for a reason."

"Shall I retrieve Winnie now, Grandmother, before I lose her?"

"You must select the *right soul* at the *right time*, child."

"I want to get out of this dreadful place, Grandmother."

"Child, it is alright for you to cry too. There is no shame in drawing upon the incredible resilience of water to help you through highly charged moments. Where answers are evasive and times are difficult, where patience has run out and the pathway ahead is little more than an act of faith, then tears are not weakness but the steeliest backbone. Most especially, when things seem hopeless, tears fuel our survival instincts and reignite our dreams. More powerful than any bone-grinding blow to an adversary, in their glittering brilliance, they fortify the spirit."

Neighbourly Loathing

Getting to know each other in the afterworlds was
Hilarious, enlightening, our companions brilliant.
Bliss in the bittersweet camaraderie of the dead.
It was all so much fun. Then one day, we cringed at
Our proximity and found it disgusting, loathsome –
And wondered what sorcery had forced us together.

Perhaps our ideals, that we could create intimate
Relationships beyond the grave, were to blame.
Maybe, the spectres of dopamine and oxytocin
Initially drew attention away from each other's
Imperfections. When these ghosts finally faded,
They let loose an abrupt sea change in our feelings
And we were revolted by the sight of each other.

We're taking things slowly now, spending a little
Time together while nurturing our own identities
And interests. Meeting in neutral spaces invites
Objectivity, but we're easily triggered. Even in death,
Trauma caused by malignant families, obstacles to love,
Paranoia, hostile beliefs and fear of intimacy, run deep.
Now, we must confront our own self-loathing, which
Through personal metamorphosis, we may yet escape.

Negative Intimacy

"Why does the cat avoid company, yet seek it, Grandmother."

"That's just cats, child. Don't read too much into it."

"But the gaping hole in its head?"

"Well, *of course* it's lost its trust in humans. The poor creature was a target for air gun practice, somewhere in the Tovil area."

"Why does it linger around Winnie so?"

"It's a contradictory creature, child. Being simultaneously dead and alive, cats always have one foot in the decomposition landscape. This particular specimen is no less decisive, and no more fond of people than any other cat. It can certainly look after itself.

"It's unnerving."

"Look not to the cat, child, but to the malevolent forces that it resists."

Games

"With a precise blow at the right angle, in the correct kind of rock, it is possible to drive a steel shaft into a limestone scabbard – thus," says Henry, making a theatrical parry with an imaginary weapon towards a limestone column.

"That is what you might initially think," says Winnie, glad of the diversion, "but there is a gentler way to persuade a sword to conceal itself in stone."

"Impossible."

"It's true. If we wrap it in a soft structure like the hem of my dress," Winnie rips a fragment off and wraps it around the invisible tip of the sword, "then drench both steel and cloth in a slow-flowing river of minerals; after a few weeks, the blade will be sheathed in stone."

Thomas spits on the ground.

"Wenches can't help but tell *tales*."

Winnie thinks to tell him about Mother Shipton's petrifying well in

Knaresborough, which sets objects into stone, but since she recalls the old woman of legend was commonly known as a witch, she thinks better of it.

"Ah well," she says, and speeds off ahead of the group. Taking a straight course across a row of stone slabs that line the base of the caves, she moves with the lightness of manner befitting a lithe, young woman.

Covetous

A feathery structure brushes Winnie's cheek. At first, she thinks it's the wren, but as another set of tiny tendrils strokes her face, she discovers they're the tips of a root system.

"A rootball! We can't be far from an exit now."

Henry rushes over to investigate, pushing his hands up high into the roof of the tunnel.

"Strewth! It's true."

Thomas lets out a piercing hoot; part battle cry, part exuberance.

Henry bear hugs Winnie as the bringer of great news and lifts her high into the air.

"Put me down, Henry! I'm getting tangled in these things."

Thomas notices Henry's bond with *the woman*. Back home, his own wife was always sullen. Although he meant only ever to please the wench, he became cruel. Contracting a wasting disease, she withered like a flower and died before they had children.

Trailing their hands against the roof of the cave, the travellers call to one another each time they feel a new rootball.

"Leave me *alone*!" shouts John, lashing out at an invisible foe.

Jim snarls protectively but cannot figure out who the aggressor is.

"Calm down, son. Calm down," says Henry, holding John's arms tightly against his body.

"I've got him," says Thomas, as he grabs the legs to stop him kicking out at Henry.

"Let me *go*!" screams John struggling against their hold.

Confused, and terrified, Jim snarls at everyone.

"Good dog," says Winnie, expertly calming the creature. "John's going to be just fine."

Following many reassurances, and a very firm grip on the scruff of the necks of both boy and dog, calm is restored.

Quickly reverting to his characteristically covert manner, John gives no excuse for the affray. Jim delightedly runs around him in eccentric circles, which earns a few sullen kicks; proof that his master is fully restored.

Communication

"Why do the rootballs bother John so, Grandmother?"

"They are speaking to him, child."

"Plants don't speak."

"Not human speech, of course. They talk with multi-species communities in the soil using chemical and electrical languages. It's obvious then, that they talk to necrobiomes and understand what each traveller will become."

"Are they part of the Compost Elevator?"

"Naturally, they boost signal efficiency, attract friendly bacteria, eavesdrop on underground electrochemical activity, distribute water, make nutrients available to those regenerating sites where they are most needed and remain vigilant to the presence to virulent bodies."

"You mean, John?"

"Indeed. His attempt to dissociate himself from the rootballs' gentle touch is his way of trying to prevent them from reading the toxic memory networks he's embedded in."

Clutching at Straws

We the desperate and dammed, are
The raw material of drastic change.
Flirting with danger, morbidity drives
Some of us to self-destruction, while
Hysteria undoes the dreams of others.
Falling under the spectre of madness,
We yearn for salvation before our souls
Begin to rot: risking everything for hope.
"Why are we doomed to this torment?"

In reckless swarms, we hurry through
The afterworlds, searching for salvation.
Visions issue from our passions but we
Cannot articulate them through words,
Signs, or expressions. While the rolling
Spring clouds hear, they can't help us:
And tatty city trash cans just don't care.
"Why are we so weak to give a damn?"

No sudden downpour, lightning bolt
Plague of locusts, or thunder marks
Our salvation. Escaping from Hell is
A drawn-out process signposted with
The stains of despair: confusion, rage,
Misery, hopelessness, shame, guilt.
We made this purgatory alone. Every
Demon lays claim to our souls tonight.
"We are ripe for transformation."

Hanging

"What's John hiding, Grandmother."

"Look to the Compost Elevator, child, to uncover such secrets."

"I don't know how to, Grandmother. Can you help me?"

"You must go much deeper than your present superficial level of understanding."

"Superficial? I've already learned how to manipulate metabolic vibrations to find my way around. I'm almost an adept."

"That's only the first stage of transitioning, child."

"Then help me reach the next."

"It is dangerous."

"I need to know if John poses a threat to the travellers, Grandmother, which endangers the retrieval process. What is he holding back?"

"You cannot influence events in the Compost Elevator."

"You've said this so many times, Grandmother, but if something malevolent is at work here then I need its true name, so I can secure the retrieval process."

"Then you must do exactly what I say, child."

"Don't I always?"

"First, you must allow yourself to be infiltrated by this space. Let the unsettling vibrations wash over you, until they are suffocating."

"What?"

"Push through the decomposition landscape. Immerse yourself in the soil."

"You want me to bury myself alive?"

"If you want access to deeper knowledge, then you must do more than to look for it. You must become part of it."

"I really don't have a choice in this, do I?"

"Breathe out. Keep breathing out."

Something chemical burns my veins. Not mortazepam, some other biologically manipulative horror, but the exhalation is therapeutic.

"Focus, child."

I pass through a rootball tendril whose wisps of organic matter sway like a pit of snakes.

"Deeper, child."

"No more chemical tricks," I say.

Suddenly surrounded by tentacles, gorgon tentacles grip my chest and pull me down into the soil.

"Stay with them longer than you think you are able to," says Grandmother.

Floundering in the deepest layers of the decomposition landscape, I soak into its substance as if I'm entirely liquid.

Revelation

Out of the decomposition landscape walks thirteen-year old Richard Taylor, who is on his way home along a woodland path. Having just collected the sum of nine shillings for his disabled father, he's tucked the money safely into a little bag that fits inside one of his mittens. As he walks, he whistles, fingering the pocket knife which his father has lent him as a treat, to cut a bow and arrow with on his way home.

John Amy Bird and James Bell, aged fourteen and eleven respectively, live nearby in a poor house and have been carefully studying Richard's routine, as he runs his precious weekly errand between Stroud and Aylesford.

"Where are you going, all pleased with yourself like that?" says John, stepping out from behind a thicket.

"I'm on my way home," says Richard.

"I like your blue jacket and waistcoat," says Jim. "It looks nice with your brown trousers and belcher handkerchief. Especially the way you wear it around your neck."

"It's nothing special," says Richard awkwardly. "Who are you two?"

A casual conversation, begins.

After a while, Richard no longer recognises the route.

"This isn't the way home," he says. "I must go back now."

"Oh, don't worry about that," says John. "This is a short cut."

"Come on. This way," says Jim.

Richard follows the brothers through the winding tracks.

"Where are we?" he begins to cry. "I've got to go home."

John springs upon him with a knife and holds it to his throat.

"Let me go!" begs the boy, "If you spare me, I'll give you all my possessions."

"That's not enough," says Jim.

"Then, I will love you forever, both of you."

John smirks.

"And I'll never tell a living soul," he sobs. "Please spare me."

The brothers quickly overpower Richard and force him down into a ditch, where John cuts his throat.

Sometime afterwards, a man named Izzard finds the boy's body, with the mitten containing the twenty shillings for his father cut from his hand. His clothes are in disarray, as if there had been a scuffle. Although his body is in a sorry state of decomposition, the bloodstains on his clothing leave no doubt about the violent nature of his death.

An immediate search for the assailant begins and the lethal weapon is identified as a commonly available white horn-handled knife, which belongs to a man named Bell, with two sons who are brought to trial for Richard's murder.

During questioning, James, the principal witness for the prosecution, produces the knife that incriminates his brother as the murderer. The jury, appalled by the lack of education and remorse shown by the brothers during the trial, immediately return a guilty verdict.

To clarify events, police take John back to the scene of the crime.

"Is this where you killed the boy, son?"

"Yes, sir," he says. "Do not you think *he is better off than I am* now?"

Despite a plea for clemency from his legal team, on account of his age and obvious lack of education, the boy is sentenced to execution in front of the new Maidstone prison. Celebrated as the most advanced model of a prison at the time, it replaces the outlying Penenden Heath as the county's execution site.

The condemned climbs a short flight of steps to the trapdoors, which are centrally supported by beams under a simple gallows rig.

"Lord have mercy upon my poor soul," says John as executioner, William Calcraft, counts down the boy's final moments on the *New Drop* scaffold and the eight thousand strong crowd attending the execution are shielded from witnessing his last struggles by a heavy, black cloth dressing on the underside of the platform.

John's body is sent to Rochester for dissection by surgeons against his wishes; a fate only fitting for criminals.

Liquid

I'm liquid because I'm crying, and I don't know how to stop.

"Although the Compost Elevator is a powerful transformer, child, which can change festering flesh into pluripotent cells, restore damaged ecologies and even mend broken hearts; it cannot convert wrong into right. Morality is the sole responsibility of the living and beyond our control in this purgatorial realm."

Cascade

The organic matter in the roof of the passageway thickens. Sensing that the density of the surrounding earth has changed, Winnie inhales deeply to sample the air.

"That aroma reminds me of coffee grounds," she says.

Henry stops and breathes in.

"Dear lady, the air around here does smell fresh and earthy but it's quite the opposite of coffee," he says, "which is an entirely disagreeable substance."

"Coffee's the scent of morning," Winnie insists.

"How can it be, when it confounds the senses even more so than the stench of tobacco," says Henry. "Besides, it's not wholesome food, it's not *good for* anything."

"It's special *because* it has such a complex character."

"Confusing," corrects Henry.

"It matures and changes during the roasting process, which confers its complexity," says Winnie. "At any point it may have a – smoky, charred, tarry, sweet, piquant, nippy, mild, delicate, sour, acrid, hard, tart, tangy, salt, soft, rough, astringent, bitter, alkaline, caustic, phenolic, creosol, enzymatic, flowery, fruity, herby, sugar-browning, nutty caramelly, chocolatey, dry distillation, carbony, spicy, or resinous character."

"That's *confusing*," says Henry.

"Maybe, but about a thousand different substances contribute to the aroma of coffee and eight hundred of those are scents, not flavours."

"You're talking nonsense, woman."

"This accounts for its richness," says Winnie. "When we try to describe 'coffee', we end up using words that do not describe the taste of the substance itself but instead refer to personal associations we make with scent and memory."

"What's the point of *that*?" says Henry.

"Well, it captures how we're feeling at any given moment."

"But, madam, that same changeability makes such a thing treacherous – these subtle *chemistries* you describe are not doing anything useful. In your own words, they encourage flights of fancy."

"They're memories," protests Winnie. "Coffee makes pleasant memories. When taken as hot drink in a relaxed environment, we indulge our favourite happy feelings. My cup of coffee is not the same as your cup of coffee but the inconstant nature of the beverage makes the experience so compelling for all of us. It's a kind of freedom to invent and enjoy a moment."

"Whatever the appeal of this fiendish bean may be," says Henry, "the coffee houses that serve it are dens of political and religious iniquity – and it's quite obvious why. With the aid of this substance, subversives gather and, assisted by these seeds of folly, plot revolution against the crown. Coffee should be banned."

"Maybe, if women weren't excluded, you'd find they were much nicer places than you propose," says Winnie.

"That's an outrageous suggestion."

They continue in silence awhile, the others dawdling in the shadows.

"I hear a waterfall," says Thomas, "but I can't make out which direction it's coming from. This place is full of echoes."

They walk on as the roof slopes downwards. It's getting much harder to for Thomas, who stoops uncomfortably low.

"Hey! These roots are loose," he says, pushing against the roof of the tunnel. "I wonder how much earth lies above us."

"Don't try and find out now," cautions Henry. "Those tethers may be the only things holding up the ground above us. If they come away, we could all be buried in an earthfall."

"On the other hand, we might get to the surface quickly," says Thomas, "and save ourselves from getting buried alive under these unstable tunnels."

They reach a dead end.

"Let's retrace our steps to the last junction," says Winnie, "and take an alternative route."

The next turning that they take is just like the last.

"I guess we try again," says Winnie.

"Another dead end," says Henry.

"Is there no way out of this hell hole?" cries Thomas, slamming his fist into the low hanging tunnel roof.

A large clod of earth tumbles into the water and everyone rushes back, as showers of soil scatter throughout the entire length of the tunnel.

"Which side of this cascade should we be on?" says Winnie.

"It's impossible to tell," says Henry, "but if we get it wrong, we won't be getting out of here at all."

The soil continues to rain down on them, until a large dome-like cavity opens above them. The travellers wait nervously to one side until the showers of earth subside.

"There's no sign of light," sighs Henry.

"Perhaps not," says Thomas, "But I can stand fully upright for the first time in ages."

He breathes in deeply.

"I can smell fresh grass here," says Thomas. "I reckon we could dig our way through if someone stands on my shoulders."

"That same person would be buried first by the downfall if it all goes wrong," says Winnie.

"We're in that place already," says Thomas with a shrug.

"I'll go," says Henry.

Winnie and John help Henry clamber on to Thomas' back. For a moment, their formation is precarious, but they soon synchronise.

"Bird. Up here." Henry flexes his fingers and the wren perches on his hand. "Okay, little chap. You're going to have to trust me. I will protect you in my open fist and push you up through the soil. If I reach open air, then I'll let you go, and you can fly away safely. If I don't, I'll keep my fist closed like a cage and bring you back safely. Will you be our canary?"

The bird eagerly agrees and disappears into Henry's hand, who plunges his fist into the soil. They wait with bated breath, and their eyes widen as Henry retracts his empty palm.

"It flew."

Winnie motions to the cat.

"You're the next smallest. It's your turn."

The cautious cat without a name that has sworn eternal distrust for humankind understands fully that it has no option but to put its fate in the hands of a man. Without further invitation, it scales the whole height of the soldiers and sits on Henry's head. Carefully, the Royalist supports the cat's weight on one hand.

"Cat. Take a deep breath. You've got work to do getting through on the other side, but with some fight, you'll make it. Ready?"

Quicker than smoke up a chimney, the cat disappears into the soil. Henry draws back his empty hand.

"He's through."

There is growing excitement from below.

"The dog."

John stands in front of Jim protectively.

"He's not going anywhere without me."

"Look, urchin," glowers Thomas. "We're doing this in a particular order. Smallest first. You wait your turn."

John defiantly glowers at the soldier.

Quickly, Winnie snatches Jim and hurls him as high as she can to Henry. Only just catching the heavy mutt by its hind leg, without explanation, the Royalist stuffs it head-first into the roof of the tunnel. It grunts like a pig and then stops.

"You've killed him," shouts John.

"Nonsense," says Henry. "Jim made it."

"Then it's my go," insists John.

"Not a chance, boy," says Thomas, pushing him firmly back and offering his linked fingers instead to Winnie as a foothold. She springs up on to his shoulders, crouches on top of Henry's back and then pushes her heels into his shoulders with all her might, kicking her legs and sweeping her arms like a swimmer through the soil.

"I'm on the other side," she says, from a place that sounds very far away. "It's amazing to be free."

"My turn!" insists John.

"There's a change of plan for the men," says Thomas. "We're each too heavy for Henry to push up by himself. So, we'll have to pull each other out."

"I'm just a boy," says John. "You can both get me through."

"Shut your bone box," says Thomas. "You're built like a man. We'll only make it if we pull each other upwards."

"You're hugger-muggers," shouts John, "both of you."

"Let's do this now, or not at all," says Henry. "Boy, you'll either work with us, or we'll do it anyway without you."

After much shouting and sulking from John, they all agree on attempting the aerial manoeuvre.

"Henry, ask the woman to pull you out," says Thomas. "Then you can reach back inside for John and me. The last man standing will be lifted to safety."

Henry leaps forcefully from Thomas' shoulders with an assisted boost by the professional soldier. His head and hands disappear into the soil and gradually his dangling feet are jerked upwards.

Thomas and John stand face to face.

"You'll lift me up now," says the boy.

"No way," says the soldier, and backs away from him. "I would be a fool to trust you."

"Loathesome fellow," screams John.

The veteran soldier keeps his cool and marks his moment. The boy howls with rage directly under the roof defect glaring at Thomas, who runs full speed at him. The man-boy's body stiffens, preparing for an assault.

Leveraging his frozen frame as a launchpad, Thomas leaps on to John's chest, using it as a stepping stone. Then he vaults high into the open earth, placing his trust in the others to catch him before he falls back to the ground.

In a drawn-out moment, Thomas disappears headfirst into the soil, hanging between escape and incarceration. Then, the dome gives way and his legs jerk skywards, as Winnie and Henry haul him inch by inch, hand over wrist, to safety.

John screams alone beneath them.

"We should help him," says Winnie.

The soldiers look at each other.

"I'm not risking my life to rescue that shabby little runt," says Thomas. "He'd have left us rot, soon as look at us."

"Then, let's tie a line of clothes together to make a rope he can climb," says Winnie.

"Though I'm loath to be bound over by moralising," says Henry, "let's give it a go."

"Do we *have* to?" says Thomas.

"We do," insists Winnie.

They knot shirts and pants into a coarse rope, which they pass back into the hole using a heavy stone as a plumb weight.

Then they feed the line into the ground.

"Careful, everyone," says Winnie, as the earth around the opening starts to sag under the weight of the stone.

The end of the rope sinks from view. Then sods of turf begin to tear and drop like a malignancy into the ground, as vibrations extend outwards from the earth underneath them and loosen the ground.

"Run!" says Henry.

They sprint away from the sinkhole, as a landslide of loose soil and rocks fills the cave complex.

Cunning Cannibals

A survival tactic,
Or an act of expedience,
Eating one's own kind is met
With disgust among humans
But is common in animals.
Unburdened by conscience,
Cannibalism is a pragmatic act;
Binding life with death
At birth, or after copulation.

Female praying mantises,
And several species of spiders,
Bite off and consume the head
Of their mate after insemination,
As enrichment for gestation.
In scorpions, who produce
Around a hundred offspring,
Some are sacrificed for food
When rations are scarce.
Nesting animals like
Rabbits and hamsters eat
Sickly, weak, or dead babies
To stave off predators that
Seek out the smell of death.

In matriphagy, mothers
Offer up their bodies,
Providing shelter for their young,
Who are forced to eat
Their way out from the inside.
Mother spider crabs leave
Unfertilized eggs for their offspring
Before their own bodies are consumed.

We the dead, with insatiable appetites,

Rachel Armstrong

Are also not bound
By the etiquette of humans.
Through repeated acts of swallowing
Each other and partial ingestions,
Metabolic networks forge our reincarnation
Through many cannibalistic acts.

Purgatory

"That hungry hole has swallowed everything, Grandmother."

"It's part of the reincarnation process. The Compost Elevator is reconfiguring the matter within its system."

"What does that mean for the travellers, Grandmother?"

"The bird has endured its painful solitude and has learned to trust in the unknown. The cynical cat remains untrusting but concedes a careful sociability with others. The dog stays loyal to its human but will be more discerning about its allegiances in the future. Thomas' toughness is softened by his own kindness, and John howls in isolation travelling a lonely path."

"Are their souls changed by this process?"

"Inevitably, child, to the point where no traces of their former selves remain."

"Why is that?"

"The re-embodying process is a gluttonous process where bodies are enfolded, each within the other."

"Doesn't that complicate things?"

"Terribly. Reincarnation is fraught with odd couplings, metabolic opportunism and shocking hybridisations. Constantly seeking to destabilise its capabilities, the Compost Elevator generates monstrous forms and hybrids. It must do so with freedom from any kind of censorship in this process, or the angels of the world would be just as unlikely as its demons."

"Then I must retrieve Winnie, Grandmother, before she's lost in this monstrous system."

"It's too late now, child. Her soul is already melding with others in the communion of life and her onward journey is already beyond the reach of soul-catchers."

"That's not true!"

"Child. Listen to me. *Hear me* now. *Winnie is not the soul you're looking for.*"

"Did you know all along, Grandmother?"

"There is no cause for concern, child. She is now set upon a natural course of reincarnation through the Compost Elevator. You must look again for the *right soul* and bring it back at the *right time.*"

In-Betweens

Our paralysis is complete: a self-replicating
Unhappiness beyond the pain and frustration of
Inconsequence, which smothers all prospects of joy.
Our salvation lies in the autonomy of exquisite filth
Writ in the redolent constituents of bodily corruption
That shapes the wasteland of the past and present.

Sick with cancer and the frustrations of everyday living,
We found each other in the cold and rain, buried at
The end of the wall where an old tree stood. Nostalgic
At first, for the cherished freedoms of earth walkers,
We were as yet unaware their alleged sovereignty was
As naught, when set against the camaraderie of the dead.

Visitors

Lizzie changes the channels with the remote-control button while staring emptily at the television.

"They may as well have taken my life as my home," she mumbles. "The other residents here are pleasant enough, but scratch the surface with conversation and they're either demented, or fools."

Her hair is tidy, she's made an effort with outdoors clothes and has tucked a book down the armchair cushion, in case her visitors are late.

"I don't want to spend the entire day asking the nursing staff for the time, or if my visitors have arrived yet," she says, impatient with the day's sloth. "I do hope they don't lose their way. Pilgrim's Way Nursing Home is hardly the centre of the universe."

Lizzie has barely opened Italo Calvino's *Cosmicomics*, when her son-in-law Joe Norris and granddaughter Jennifer arrive.

"So, how are you doing, Lizzie?" says Joe, as he hands her a brown paper bag of freshly-washed grapes.

"Not bad," says Lizzie.

Jennifer does not say much, as she's trying to ignore the voices.

Everyone's watching you (whispering).

Any kind of reading, like studying for her A-levels, helps the voices dull-down, but anything mundane, including everything that her family talks about, sends them raving.

"Hello, Grandmother," she mumbles against the old woman's cheek, then turns her back and opens a text book.

It's hard for Jennifer to accept that the frail old woman in the chair is the same person who used to take her out for walks on Penenden Heath when her parents wanted to spend *happy* Sundays together.

Back then, Lizzie had a good eye and a keen mind for things.

"Do you remember the strange tooth we found while walking, Jenny?" says Lizzie.

Although Jennifer says nothing, she remembers the incident clearly.

The strange object looked like a stone at first glance and before Lizzie could examine it properly, Jenny's little fingers had picked it up out of the dirt.

"Oh goodness," said Lizzie, "that's a tooth."

"For the fairies?"

"Oh no. They won't like that one. It's an old and rotten thing," says Lizzie. "Put it down, or it will bring all kinds of nasty stuff back into the house."

Jenny had never seen a fairy tooth before and couldn't leave it behind. When she thought Lizzie was watching, she made-pretend to throw it back down on the ground, but secretly slipped it into her coat pocket instead.

Her, her, her (laughing).

Those were the good old days when Lizzie was sprightly, and the voices weren't there.

"Speak to me, Jenny," says Lizzie. "You've come all this way. Tell me what you're thinking about."

The young woman smiles, wanting to bring the conversation around to reading, and make the voices quieten down.

"What is *Cosmicomics* about? Granny?" she says.

That's all you think about.

"I don't know, dear. I haven't started it yet. I think it's going to be amusing, though. Don't you? It says so in the title."

They're all laughing at you.

Jennifer shrugs. She doesn't find the cosmos 'amusing', as her ambition is to set foot on an alien world, perhaps the Moon, or Mars.

"Pass it to me and I'll let you know," says Jennifer, relieved to be back in the company of a book.

Joe announces that it's time to leave, just as she finishes the hundredth page and hands it back to Lizzie.

"What did you think of it, dear?"

You can't tell fact from fiction, you're so stupid.

"I'm not finished yet."

"Well, what's your initial impression, then?"

"It's not *proper* science, but I think *you'll* like it, Granny."

Lizzie settles down happily with her book, losing herself in a strange universe for the rest of the evening.

"The excruciating joy of having relatives over to visit," she says to the staff nurse, who comes to close her book and turn off the light around two in the morning, "is not to argue with them, but to find ways of indulging their company. Nobody wants to die lonely."

Resentment

"It's *not fair*! You could have *told* me that Winnie wasn't the *right soul.*"

"Your emotions are getting the better of you, child."

"I need to know such *important* things."

"You must figure them out for yourself, child. It's part of the learning process."

"When my own soul is on the line, I do not want to learn afterwards that the risks I took were entirely unnecessary."

"You'll get used to it, child. Doing *nothing* is also not without risk."

"I won't get *used to it*, no matter how you obfuscate the whole process."

"Of course, child, but you really mustn't let your emotions cloud your judgement."

The nausea I'm feeling is too familiar.

"Put your damned potions away, Grandmother," I mumble as the mortazepam kicks in, "I will handle this *my way.*"

Hitchhikers Nine

The sky cracks like an eggshell burst by lightning.

They've just reached a set of traffic lights over the Maidstone bridge complex and Will needs to make sure he's in the right lane, before heading out of the town centre in the Rochester Road direction. With the Old Palace in his rear-view mirror again, he shakes his head.

More light fractures the sky.

Winnie's substance rapidly fades and the young woman can see the upholstery pattern through her skin.

The next moment, the old woman is expunged in a flash of brightness.

"What on earth possessed you to be out and about on such a dreadful night?" says Will.

No reply comes from the back seat, so he checks the rear-view mirror.

His passenger looks so incredibly sad that he leaves her to her thoughts.

Book Two
Jennifer

Part V: Reincarnation

Think of the little material body, called an egg, and think of the enormous and very complex material body, say, an elephant, that may come out of it: here you have a permanent stream of materializations before your eyes, all of them occurring in the way of assimilation, of a spreading entelechial control.

– Hans Driesch

Swimming

"I'm off to find Winnie," I say."

"You don't need my permission, child," says Grandmother, "you're an adept now."

The moment I start to search for her I am swallowed by a sudden darkness, which compresses my vibrations until the strain is unbearable. In a surge of relief, I am suddenly expelled through a viscous membrane.

My heightened sense of touch serves me well in this lightless space and I start to run. The ground is spongy, and I can feel the gaze of a million souls gathering like a cloud around me. Some try to reach me weakly from the depths of this fuzzy space, while others make their *presence* known to me from nearby.

"Pick me. *Pick* me. Pick *me*," they insist.

"Winnie!" I call, but my vibrations are carried away by a persistent, whispering wind that won't stop talking over me.

I stumble on.

The ground becomes boggy and it's much harder going. Many more souls pack themselves into the space around me, our intensity of purpose generating an uncomfortable pressure.

"Pick me. *Pick* me. Pick *me*," they refrain.

Gravity is working against me. Or, is it the trick of the swamp? – that one step forwards is really several backwards, or downwards. I can't tell.

I force my way through the crush of souls clinging to my empathy.

I can't let them weigh me down.

"Winnie," I call, but my words are mere vibrations, hijacked by my so many dogged *others* here. Each have a name, none of which I remember, and all are begging me to take their soul back to the living realm.

They're making so much noise that Winnie could be everywhere, or nowhere.

"Pick me. *Pick* me. Pick *me*," chants the discordant chorus.

I'm crawling through soft mud, soil and slush now. Everything's holding me back, sucking at my progress, stifling my resolve.

The weight of the souls clinging to me is more than I can carry.

I fall.

Chicken and Egg

"I'm astonished by your naiveté, child." Says Grandmother. "It's clear you know nothing about the radical transformational potential of the Compost Elevator."

"Right now, Winnie's soul must be searching for a host body to attach to, Grandmother."

"Let her go, child. The dead are kith to each other. This is not to say that their lives mingle in straight lines, or through obvious causalities. Rather, their trajectories should be regarded as alternative forms of existence, which defy dualistic gridlocks like chicken-and-egg – body and soul."

"So, I may still find her?"

"Transformation is so much more than the processes of death, and has more to do with how the webs of reincarnation are forged."

"You mean how compost is formed?"

"No. The Compost Elevator is *far more* than the formation of soil."

"How *can* this be?"

"Its principles are retained by reorganising matter, which become entangled with the webs of life."

"It's inside *living* bodies?"

"Of course, how do you think development, adaptation, metamorphosis and reincarnation are possible?"

"*Life* doesn't need your Compost Elevator."

"Then living bodies would never change. Eggs would make eggs and chickens would produce only chickens."

"You're twisting things around again, Grandmother. You know that chickens make eggs, and eggs make chickens."

"You are creating paradoxes where there are none, child. Doubtlessly, you'll have asked yourself, which one comes first?"

"Naturally, there's an order."

"It depends on your perspective. I assume you regard an egg as a specific life-object that is distinct from a chicken-object and vice versa."

"A chicken is not an egg."

"By taking this polar perspective, you erase the continuity between them, and with it their capacity for transformation."

"How do you mean?"

"When you consider things in terms of absolute categories, one item cannot be turned into another. If there are slippages within the status of an object, then more categories must be invented to signify this change by referring to discrete stages like egg, embryo, foetus, chick, pullet, adult, corpse."

"How does the Compost Elevator resolve this conundrum?"

"It understands that entanglements exist across the whole spectrum of life. The relationship between chickens and eggs is a continuous, but not always gradual, process that is rich with developmental twists, punctuations and flourishes."

"This doesn't *change anything*, Grandmother."

"It ends the *idea* the living world is made up of idealised bodies, and in this way, the Compost Elevator is free to seize every opportunity it can to persist, using any available range of physiological events, environmental conditions and anatomical structures. So, non-chickens, proto-chickens and post-chickens, are all in a dynamic relationship with their chicken-ness…"

"Or, egg-ness."

"Right, child, they are all possible expressions of bodies that are not always alike – but empathetically recognise each other."

"Oh, hang on. You mean an egg, or a chicken could produce something *else*?"

"Of *course*, they can. The Compost Elevator has a lot of 'spare capacity' for making bodies through all kinds of unlikely alliances."

"Then, Winnie could become *something else*?"

"Of *course* she could."

"Where does this transformation take place then, in the soil?"

"No, child, within life-organising systems like the allantois, chorion, amnion, egg sac and placenta."

"You mean reproductive systems?"

"Naturally. The Compost Elevator extends into the material systems that support the transformation of the primitive and diffusely spread soul substance. Entering into a new stage of vitalisation that starts at the fertilisation process, the proto-soul is concentrated and matured within the developing body by various life-organising systems. Pulsing with liquid protocols, the different maternal systems guide the synthesis of emerging states of being through manifolds of material organisation. As the early pluripotent tissue masses are organised into various spatial configurations, their twists, rolls and folds further strengthen the soul substance. As one set of negotiations is completed, another begins by differentially introducing time, space and complexity into embryonic developmental pathways. Gradually, these enfleshings form recognisable tissues and organs, which are capable of supporting a self-regulating being. These principles are almost the inverse of the soils you're familiar with. While soils release the soul substance from a body and break down matter for assimilation by organic systems, maternal structures condense souls and reorganise them within matter to produce highly specific new lifeforms."

"When is the soul recognisable during this process?"

"That's a controversial issue, child. Like bodies, souls are neither fully formed, nor complete. Being protean, they are uniquely and continually shaped by their encounters with others, and their experience of the world."

"Could I be ensnared by this reincarnation system, Grandmother?"

"It presents a significant risk to you, child. If you become entwined with the developing embryonic matter within, then you will be set on a specific pathway of incarnation, from which I'll not be able to bring you back."

Homeless

The *game* of fertilisation *is told*
By the living, as a story where
The egg passively waits for the
Fittest from millions of sperm
To cross the finish line. Thanks
To missing, or deformed tails,
Strange heads, odd midpieces,
Poor motivation and other defects,
Plenty don't even introduce themselves.
Others get snared in sticky fluid
Lining the reproductive tract that
Stops all but the strongest swimmers.
In this tale, the winner takes all in
One last sprint to the end, where
The egg graciously receives the
First random partner she meets.
In another version of events,
Championed by *the realms of*
The dead, the seductress egg is
Not a submissive, undiscerning
Receptacle, but an equal and active
Player in the art of reproduction.
Sometimes predatory, she crafts
Layers of evolutionary control
Around her domain, wooing
Sperm with specific genes and
Shaping the character of the
Tiny life-form she chooses to raise.

In Parallel

"Where am I, Grandmother? I can't get my bearings on this place."

"That's hardly surprising, child. You're transitioning between worlds and parallel realities are at play."

The decomposition landscape here is so dense.

I push my way into an increasingly viscous realm, where hosts of vagrant souls are trying to draw my attention. I pass through them, as if I were browsing stalls in a bazaar.

"Pick me. *Pick* me. Pick *me*," they say.

"You're letting ambient noise distract you, child. Focus, and start again."

"I want to know how these systems work."

"Life-organising structures use all the same material building blocks as soils – carbon, hydrogen, oxygen, phosphorous, sulphur, nitrogen – but capture different *kinds* of stories, soul distillations and environmental vibrations, and draw them together through different choreographies of matter. Don't assume for a moment this process is logical or fathomable. They are highly contrary."

"Why so?"

"They have deep and surprising origins."

"How do you mean?"

"Let's start with the nature of the placenta, which is not entirely 'mammalian'."

"It's the very definition of a *mammal*."

"It evolved from a sexually transmitted cloacal infection in early mammals around 250 million years ago. Syncytial retroviruses integrated their viral codes and linked different cell types together in the infected area, forming a simple organ capable of supplying developing embryos with food from the mother. Being so close to the germ line, this know-how was passed into the genes of the next generation, where embryos snuggled deep in the mother's pelvis. Here, they slept safely until the moment of birth, when the semi-autonomous new-born was forced to make a lightning shift from a liquid existence to the air."

"Extraordinary," I say. "The Compost Elevator truly is a realm of monsters."

Leaky

When the first complex cells
Started to infect and transform
Each other as populations of
Cooperating diverse bodies, the
Compost Elevator consolidated
these relationships, giving rise
To the *eukaryotic* domain of life.

Education

"Where are you now, child?" says Grandmother, who feels very far away.

"I'm high above the Invicta Grammar School in Maidstone, where, within the walls of the sand-brick modern building, a powerful young soul is demanding my attention."

Crush

Rain streams down the classroom window and puddles out along the sills. Jennifer Norris dreams of designing self-sustaining habitats, or 'mini worlds', and pulls her cardigan sleeves over her hands, like gloves.

"Alien", she writes with a finger on the foggy condensate creeping up the pane.

You'll never be anyone. What a waste of time you are.

Today's exercise is all about chemical formulae and balancing equations, which is creatively algebraic. Since she's already got the hang of the homework exercises and the voices have let her alone, she thinks about Peter Mitchell.

While they live in the same neighbourhood around the Boughton Lane area, they don't go to the same school. She's at Invicta Grammar School, which is located along the Ashford Road area just on the outskirts of Maidstone, while he's at the Valley Park School, which is close by.

Happily, their journeys coincide, and Jennifer has been watching his comings and goings from a distance.

Recently, Peter spoke to her when alighting from the bus at the town centre.

"After *you*," he said, nonchalantly.

"After you… after you are wasting your time. You, stupid girl. You should be studying," say the voices, as she smiles at Peter.

Mostly, if she waits, they'll quieten down. Then, she'll look around to see if people are talking normally. Annoyingly, the voices interrupt her when she's thinking about other things and never tell her anything that she doesn't already think or know. Over the years, she's regarded them as *classroom chatter*. Sometimes it's not benign but confusing and she can't actually tell whether someone really is talking about her, to her, or not at all. When she can't be sure, she stays silent, and waits for things to *declare themselves*.

A sheet of equations is passed around for homework.

(Whispering). What a waste of time you are. Wasting time. Always wasting it.

She stares at the page, unable to focus on the instructions as Peter's tousled nut-brown hair, sun-kissed skin and large blue eyes join the phantoms in her thoughts.

You just daydream. You'll never get his attention.

Jennifer hates their intrusiveness and nagging. Sometimes they sound like a television has been left on somewhere, and at other times they're more muted, like the voices in a railway station. Occasionally, she recognises them as extreme caricatures of her own thoughts and anxieties. These are the most unsettling, as they confront her with uncomfortable truths and question her grasp of reality.

What are you going to do about it?

Union

The voices are making Jennifer miserable. Her crush on Peter is a constant, intense source of torment, which is exploited by a particularly harrowing, older woman's voice.

You're worthless.

"I'm better than *you*."

Peter goes out with all kinds of girls but does not appear to be going steady with anyone in particular. This is a good sign, and if Jennifer works hard enough on her appearance, perhaps she could show him what an excellent date she'd make. Not that she knows much about dating, but she figures it's time to make a start.

Do something to get his attention.

"I'm doing *everything* I can."

Viewing their potential relationship as achievable through a series of logical moves, she's scheduled her route to school to coincide with Peter's movements.

Try harder.

"I *am* trying harder."

She knows what his preferred route is, where he likes to sit on the bus, what days he appears to come home early for a study day and even what kind of date he prefers. Being organised is the best way she can deal with people, so she can ignore the voices making suggestions to the contrary.

Prove that you want him. Hurt yourself.

"I won't do that. I'll find my own way."

First, she identifies ways of meeting him more often. It takes eight conversations before someone starts to consider you a friend. Fortunately, owing to the proximity of the campuses, there is plenty of opportunity for their paths to cross.

If you really want him, you'll hurt yourself. Go on. Hurt yourself.

"Leave me alone. You're *so* annoying."

The calculated opportunities appear to be working, and Jennifer moves into the second phase of her plan. She talks to Peter regularly, sometimes while taking shelter together from the constant rain at the bus stop. During a particularly sudden and heavy downpour, he lifts his Barbour over their heads.

"Hello! Remember me?" says Jennifer cheerily.

"Sure, what was your name?"

"I'm Jenny. If you hold that end of the coat, we can make it to that covered doorway together."

"Okay, then."

Everyone is looking at you.

"I don't care."

Peter looks puzzled. Jennifer smiles awkwardly.

The third phase of her plan moves from being friendly faces that pass greetings, to establishing a 'serious' relationship.

What the fuck are you even trying to do?

"Who are you? Get out of my head."

Call me by my true name, bitch.

"Get lost. I don't know you."

Jennifer's methodological approach keeps her anxieties at bay and her confidence steadily grows. One afternoon they sit together under a porch outside, watching a blocked guttering drench passers waiting for a bus that doesn't seem to be coming. Within a couple of months, they are occasional 'kissing friends'.

Annoyingly, Peter continues to see other girls.

Stupid girl, he doesn't want you.

"Leave me alone."

Like the female attention that Peter frequently receives, Jennifer ignores all the intrusions. Girls seem to have a habit of bumping into him accidentally on purpose on the bus, or talking in ridiculously loud voices and even spilling drinks on him. However, her competitive instincts are roused when she overhears in the canteen that he's been making out with Kate and is also seeing Cheryl.

Those other girls are so much more attractive than you are.

"Shut up."

I will hurt you.

"You will not. You're just a stupid voice."

Your mouth is metal and the air bitter acid.

"Ouch! The pain in my teeth!

I can cause pain in any part of your body. All I have to do is name it.

"Make it stop. Please, make it stop."

Then, do as you're told.

Every time she hears the old woman's voice, Jennifer feels particularly wretched.

Show that you want him. Or I'll give you a pain in your head. You know what I'm talking about, bitch.

"Shut up. Just shut up."

Slamming all the doors as she makes her way to her bedroom, Joe calls up after her, which makes her headache worse.

"What's up, Jenny?"

Crying herself to exhaustion and refusing her parents' calls to come and have dinner, Jennifer finally wipes her swollen eyes and stares at her collection of things, which mark all the important events in her childhood. There's her battle worn flat pink ted, dressed as an astronaut, with its bare patches of fur that have been darned over with wool that doesn't quite match. There's the fish bowl she's turned into a terrarium. Here, are the cut glass beads she used to swap as treasure through which she could view multiple worlds. These are the five fossils that Joe bought her from a precious stone shop in Hastings, which spoke of completely different forms of life during the Cambrian Explosion, when all the world's body-parts were formed. And here is the tooth-stone that she forgot to throw away on Penenden Heath.

She picks it up. In the fading light, it seems to speak to her, the fragile apatite surface bewitchingly pulsing yellow and purple hues.

What are you going to do about it?

"Nothing!"

I'm going to teach you a lesson. I won't go away until you know yourself better. Nor will the pain in your stomach.

She's nauseous all night and the voice doesn't settle down. It's still there in the morning, calling out body parts – her *head*, her *stomach*, her *eyes* – so that she's unable to think properly.

Do what I say or kill yourself.

"You're evil," cries Jennifer, "I won't self-harm," but the voice won't back down.

Address me by my name, bitch. Unless you show me what you're prepared to do for him, you don't deserve to live. Kill yourself, or fuck him. Your choice. Show me what you're made of.

Peter, who has begun to look forward to Jennifer's company, agrees to meet her at the Maidstone Cemetery on their way home. He usually enjoys her bright and charming conversation. Although she's not the prettiest girl he's dated, she always has something interesting to say and do. Today, she seems agitated.

"Let's make out in the triangle wood at the far end of the cemetery," says Jennifer, who shows she has brought an umbrella and a condom.

"Well, I'm flattered but…"

"You *have* to," says Jennifer, "please, you absolutely *have* to."

She's glancing distractedly.

I'll cause you untold pain if you back down. I'll make you kill yourself.

"Jenny, are you okay?"

Pressured by the degree of preparation, resolution and commitment to the deed, Peter finally agrees to execute her plan textbook style, as if they were on the *Discovery Channel.*

When they're done, the young couple are subdued.

Why did you let me tell you what to do?

You've ruined everything.

Everything's ruined.

Stupid girl.

Slut.

Jennifer's head is throbbing; her stomach hurts and it's too hard to ignore the horrid voice.

You shouldn't let him take advantage of you.

Look what you did to yourself.

A pain in your stomach.

Pain behind your eyes.

Pain in your soul.

Stupid girl.

Slut.

"Why don't you just *fuck off!*"

Peter straightens his clothes, nods and leaves.

Look how low you'll stoop to get what you want.

"I didn't want this!" Jennifer shouts back at the voice, at Peter, then, beats the ground with her fists.

You should use my name, bitch.

I'm teaching you how to get to know yourself better.

"I don't know who the hell you are!".

All the way home, she tries to stop the voice from calling out her body parts and threatening her with horrible smells. Finally, she figures that by working as hard as possible, she can sufficiently downstage the commands but her resolute concentration is no remedy for her blossoming friendship with Peter having been turned into something terrible.

Shutting her feelings out, she spreads her biology books across her bedroom.

Loser.

"Things will be all right again."

Of course, she could not be more wrong.

Desperate Attraction

Empathy is a delightful treasure,
Which unites us with the living world.
Through it, we are semi-permeable
To emotional landscapes, capable of
Absorbing the feelings of others,
Which strengthen our capacity for
Self-reflection. Confronting ourselves,
We can examine and amend our faults.

Empathy is an elixir craved by
Emotionally crippled souls, addicted
To attention. Delighting in chaos, they
Forge traumatic bonds, becoming
Cold and withholding affection from us
To establish an upper hand in a turbulent
Sea of cruelty and emotional manipulation.

Empathy steadies the path and raises
Our hopes, when we're abused for our
Kindness and care. Holding the rudder
In a sea of insincerity, littered with troughs
Of persecution and false reassurances,
It helps us withstand the damage wrought
Upon us; the push and pull of malignant
Souls that stop us leaving them, in safety.

Empathy is the voice that one day says,
"We can't help you. Not everyone heals,
We're letting you go."

Immersion

"Give me a clue about what I'm looking for," I say, being sucked down further and deeper into the soggy space.

Things are definitely messier when you're an adept.

"If you paid more attention to what's actually there, rather than trying to guess what should be there, you'd find what you're looking for sooner," says Grandmother.

My contempt for these 'games' has no limits, so I plunge right into the gooey substance that now clings to every aspect of my being.

It's vibrating, porous, like a soft gauze around me.

The voices of souls are there, but so very faintly I can barely feel them.

Rapidly, I become entangled in the fabric as it creeps, rises from the ground and puts forth tentacles like an amoeba. At times, it seems as if it's coming from my own form, while at others it's radiating around me like an aura.

"What *is* this substance?" I ask.

"It's the materialising bridge between the spirit and the body," says Grandmother. "Some call it *ectoplasm*."

Speck

Within the sticky muck.

I detect.

A speck.

An imperceptible ort of life.

Despite the fumbling attempts at contraception, in defiance of social conventions, regardless of the wrong people, an improper place, at an inconvenient time, for all the wrong reasons and in entirely the wrong way – here's a speck.

Against the odds.

The chances of life forming by random processes alone based on the possibility of the random synthesis of a small protein is said to be less than one in ten to the power of forty thousand. In other words, the odds against life happening by accident are greater than once in thirteen billion years – the age of the universe.

Life should not exist.

An accident.

And yet, a dot of life.

Here.

"Grandmother," I shout. "There are signs of life."

Biological Accidents

"Life is not an 'accident', child. Wipe yourself clean of that stuff. It's causing all kinds of interference patterns in your bio-traces."

"It's hard to get off."

"Life does not flourish or diversify by making *errors*."

"How do you mean, Grandmother?" I say, remembering something to the contrary. "At times of stress, nature *prefers* mistakes."

"Don't be ridiculous. They're not mistakes, child."

"What's *your* version of events?"

I'm oddly relaxed by the presence of the lingering plasm. Grandmother's intense musings are reverberating through my thoughts, as if I'm in a swimming pool.

"The conventional story of life relies on accidents to produce variety where, at the moment of fertilisation, the fusion of sex cells sets a 'genetically determined' sequence in motion. Governed by biological codes, the construction of a new organism is orchestrated from the fundamental building blocks of proteins, fats, carbohydrates, minerals and vitamins – a biochemical assembly line that moves towards ideal, repeatable configurations. The same processes are repeated time after time, through generations of creatures until 'errors' happen. These so-called faults in the system, are then 'silently' passed down to offspring and, when the circumstances are 'right', they are favourably selected to confer a creature with competitive advantage compared with its peers. Over time, these differences make new species and lineages. In this sense, the whole process of diversity and evolution is understood as an *elegant mistake*."

"What's so wrong with this *accidental* nature?" I say.

A faint strand of plasm wraps itself around me in an endless knot.

"It is not specific enough. Error itself cannot account for the degree of difference and creativity that we see in nature."

"Why ever not?"

The plasm slips around my wrist and disappears completely from view.

"Mistakes are mistakes, child. Any system that proposes to deal with the changing world by making 'errors', is not viable by definition. Besides, creatures have a whole range of strategies to prevent 'mistakes', such as tissue repair, immune systems and adaptive behaviours. We are not 'here' *by* error, *we persist despite it* and we do so through life's effusive creativity where we are actively tuned to our habitats through the *process of living*."

"Surely, that's the same thing?"

The ectoplasm makes my skin tingle pleasantly and as I pull it from me it forms strands of white smoke-like substance that rise in twisting shapes.

"It's completely different. Error is not a strategy, *creative tolerance* is."

"What's the difference?"

"Life achieves its goals in various ways, if it is to deal with the many surprises that the real world brings, then it must be able to work beyond a body's limits and stay relevant to its surroundings."

"How does it manage that?"

"It maintains this active ongoing conversation through *metabolism*, not genetics. These active cell processes link a body to its surroundings and even make the final decisions about how the processes of life and death are carried out."

"We should be as nebulous as clouds, then," I say, "as our bodies would simply merge with our surroundings, like in compost."

Thread-like strands of plasm burst into fine, airborne bodies, like seeds on a dandelion clock.

"That metabolic systems are radically open does not mean that *anything goes*, child. In life, all living systems are constrained by many factors – from the laws of chemistry, to the nature of their niches and their relationships with other beings. The Compost Elevator allows many degrees of freedom, so creatures can mount highly creative responses to all kinds of circumstances, even enabling them to suspend their active lives through hibernation, or sporulation."

"And many bodies have died, or gone extinct, during this process."

The plasm is streaming now, rising like a shimmering mirage within which I can see all kinds of bodily forms.

"In the Compost Elevator, child, 'death' is not a waste of a life but a way of making new organisms through the continual mixing and merging of life's fields. Think of it as a *living cloud* of potential that permeates a range of material interfaces. It presence provokes those events that give rise to beings, memories, souls, encounters, relationships, traumas, exchanges, dreams and hopes for the future."

"Then the Compost Elevator is truly a *comedy of errors*," I say, distracted by the writhing ocean of forms in which I am immersed and feeling inexplicably cheery. "All those fundamental misunderstandings I've come across here may not be 'errors' at all then, in *your version of events*, but symptoms of life's irrepressible creativity."

All the marvellous things cavorting before me suddenly disappear.

"Life, death, comedy and tragedy are not polar opposites, child, but complementary ways of being and experiencing the world. This is exactly what makes up the richness of life."

"If you say so."

"Take, for example, the misplaced intentions of two teenagers at a crossroads between the living and the dead that unwittingly invite these realms to mingle. Not just through the unintended side effects of inexpertly used contraception but also because their tragic act is performed in a graveyard – exactly where the old life forces are most strongly drawn towards new ones. Inevitably, familiar boundaries are being transgressed, provoking more creativity, so that otherwise unrelated events are starting to infuse one another with fresh potential."

Entanglements With the Dead

The thresholds of the afterworlds separate
Us from *them*. Viewed from the *other* side,
Death reinvigorates vagrant souls, whose
Evolution is more than the sum of exchanges
Between the living and dead. Not cancelling
Each other out, but coming-together through
Many disparate bodies, which furthers the
Planet's self-renewal. Such exchanges, are rich
With new insights and forge the cycles of life.

Growing

A sweet spot within the ectoplasm partially liquefies, allowing me to approach it.

It doesn't have a name a shape or character yet, but it's 'there'. I think it's smiling at me.

"I want to live," it says.

A sudden swell of thick goo forms a 'wall' of matter through which I can no longer approach or pass.

I try moving towards the place where I last felt its vibrations and a flurry of souls gathers around my empathy.

I know it's there *somewhere*, but these other presences are keeping it from me.

"Pick me. *Pick* me. Pick *me*," says the cloud of souls.

I don't want *them*.

I want *you*, my little soul.

Inconstant

Hoping to meet Peter at the usual time by the bus stop, Jennifer wonders if she should leave her hair up, tuck it stylishly under a waterproof hat, or shake it loose.

Gave yourself away so easily. Slut.

"Stop it."

Maybe, there's a chance to make up.

What do you think you look like?

"I really don't care."

She doubles down in her defiance by making no effort in her appearance.

He doesn't want someone like you.

Taking a seat at the side of the classroom, she has a clear view of everyone in the physics lesson.

"Today's open discussion will about the Fermi Paradox," says Miss

Jones. "Does anyone know what that is?"

Jennifer raises her pencil. The teacher nods, encouragingly.

"It's the contradiction between the likelihood of life existing in the cosmos and lack of evidence confirming it."

An exchange follows where various classmates discuss what aliens actually look like. Jennifer has to work hard to see who's speaking and make sure she's hearing her classmates, not the voices.

Thinks she's so smart but we know what you did.

You make us sick.

"Shut up."

Some girls suggest extra-terrestrials are like the 'greys' – thin and elegant pale humanoids beings -- others say they're like animals on Earth, but with many limbs and eyes to cope with different kinds of environmental conditions. A conversation about *weird slime*, something that Miss Jones calls "biofilms", begins.

"Alien life is not *like us* by definition," says Jennifer. "It's unlikely to be similar to anything we currently recognise. You're all just re-presenting versions of life on Earth."

"Go on," encourages Miss Jones.

"It's impossible to discover alien life when we don't actually know what we're looking for. Even on Mars, any life that evolved was most likely so primitive it was still bound to the rocks before the planet became inhospitable. If that is the case, then we should be looking at rocks, not for free-living creatures. Besides, these things are likely to be absolutely tiny. We certainly wouldn't see them with the naked eye. Even if we were searching for a creature the size of a blue whale, in the vastness of the cosmos, we'd still never be able to find it with our current instruments."

"What do you suggest instead?" says Miss Jones.

Everyone's laughing at you.

Jennifer looks briefly around the classroom to make sure nobody is laughing.

"We should be looking for water and alien soils around Goldilocks Zones of exoplanets. We need to first identify life-promoting conditions before we start to think about what specific creatures might emerge from them. Based on Kepler space mission data, there could be as many as forty billion Earth-sized planets orbiting in the habitable zones of Sun-like stars and red dwarfs in the Milky Way. Eleven billion of them may even be orbiting Sun-like stars. We haven't got the resolution to see alien pond scum or creatures with lots of legs, or anything like that. Not yet. So, if we think about the Fermi Paradox not in terms of trying to observe life but finding the terrains that increase the probabilities of life, then it's not a paradox at all. We're taking a much wider perspective, and as a result, we've already found lots of hotspots."

"You've *solved* the Fermi Paradox, then?"

"The question *what is life* is still wide open. I'm just saying we can hardly be surprised if we've not found evidence of a manifestation of life that we've preconceived. Our present instruments simply aren't capable of delivering the kind of detail and evidence to confirm, or disprove, the proposed paradox. If life elsewhere in the universe is important to us, then surely we should be trying to make it happen."

"What do you mean by that, Jennifer?" says Miss Jones.

"We must seed life forms we recognise on planets we can observe. Then, we will know exactly what we are looking for, as well as standing a chance of confirming their signatures. If we can prove that hardy life forms can thrive in space, then we can develop better instruments and approaches to establish whether the paradox is true or not."

Everyone knows your dirty secrets.

Jennifer looks around to see who is talking.

"Why don't we look to the problems on our own planet first, before we go invading some poor alien ecology with our nasty bacteria?" says Kate, who is irritated that Peter's mentioned her name favourably a few times when they've been dating. "Your thinking is typically human-centric. It's know-it-alls, like you, that are killing this planet with misplaced ambitions."

"I tell you what," says Jennifer. "Why don't you stay at home and fix the world's problems, while I go and establish a terrestrial life-centred community around the cosmos. Whether the challenges that beset our planet are picket-fence tidy or not, we will reach a point, at around two to three billion years from now, when Earth enters a hot zone. At that point, our oceans will evaporate, and complex life will be untenable. So, rather than *people like me*, it's *people like you* who will ensure the end of human civilisation. You're unable to think beyond the status quo, so you hide behind your lack of ambition and creativity, to justify your inaction. What's misplaced, is that you do this under the guise of morality."

They all hate you, you know.

Jennifer looks a little too intensely at Kate, trying to figure out if her

175

lips are still moving.

"It's all very well, shooting bacterial bullets at the stars," says Cheryl, who hangs out with Kate, "but you'll also be sowing the seeds of human destruction way before the natural death of our planet."

"I'm sure going extinct the 'natural' way is very romantic," says Jennifer. "I personally, prefer not to go extinct at all. Of course, it is possible our species could be inadvertently wiped out if things go wrong, but it is certain that humanity will be extinct if we choose to do nothing. By definition, doing *something* involves risks. The sensible thing is to properly assess whether those risks are worth taking or not. Just like Kate, you're hiding behind a fatalistic standpoint because you can't envisage an effective alternative. Then, you sweeten the blow by calling it 'natural'."

"Nature's a fact." says Cheryl.

"Nature is something we invent. And invention is at the heart of why we're still here at all on the planet. It's certainly not down to fate's good grace."

"You're ridiculous. Nature's real, it's out there – beyond the window, not in your books. I bet you can't imagine that. And you're talking about timescales that are even bigger than your ego," says Cheryl. "Other things may come up in the meantime, which will give us different options, you brainiac."

Lies, you're telling lies.

"Get lost!"

"Let's not make this personal, girls," warns Miss Jones.

"Like what? Be specific about these imaginary *soft options*. At least I try to tackle difficult concepts and if you read more, then you'd already know that our own 'natural' living systems could be seeded from elsewhere in the solar system. Meteorites carrying alien molecules probably began the origin of life, in a process called *panspermia*."

"So what?"

"So, if nature itself is alien. The morality your argument assumes is highly questionable. Directed panspermia is just another way of making nature."

"We don't *make* nature," says Kate.

"If we can't, then it's pointless sending human colonies into space, as we're going to have to build earth-like ecosystems to support them."

"So, what would you *build* nature with, then, brainiac?"

"Microorganisms. They were the first life here, and their living processes have practically forged the conditions for all life on this planet."

"That's *your* idea of *nature*," says Kate.

"Microorganisms are hardier than we are, more metabolically robust and present us fewer ethical dilemmas in their deployment on one-way missions, which I know you all deeply care about. Without microbes, we're not going anywhere. Our own advancement in the cosmos can only be achieved in partnership with other life forms, so we need to get good at making nature. That means we need to start directing our panspermia experiments right now."

"A puddle of sludge isn't 'nature'," chimes in Kate.

(Whispering). You think you know it all, know-it-all.

"Shut up"

"Stick to the facts, girls," says Miss Jones.

Jennifer looks at Kate, Cheryl then the rest of the class. Their lips are still.

"It's not, on Earth, because we need more than one organism to survive but we call the shots on whether something is nature or not, as it's a culturally defined term. The first seedling extra-terrestrial ecologies would be simple at first, perhaps like pond scum or lichens on stones, and they would have to be managed in some way. But, given these propositions, we can now say what alien life 'might' be. We can start to meaningfully discuss the Fermi paradox because we've got some knowledge of the starting conditions. However we go about it, we actually need do something effective about ensuring the long-term survival of our species. If so, we have to go beyond these preliminary debates, as we are simply running out of time."

You're mad.

"I'm not."

The voices are playing up and Jennifer is finding it difficult to tell exactly who is being derogatory.

Stupid slut.

"Stop it."

She looks around to see who might be discussing her.

"Right girls, that's enough. I've got a sheet with homework questions. Given the vigour of this debate, a few of you might even enjoy the set question today, which was designed by the British Interplanetary

Society's Space Science and Technology A-level initiative. Essentially, it's asking for your ideas on what it would take to set up a successful habitat on the Moon."

At the bus stop, Jennifer waits for Peter, passing the time by tying her hair back and then, letting it loose again. Four buses pass and still there is no sign of him.

A vintage orange Nissan GT with tailfin and blinged-out twenty-eight-inch wheels pulls up and a youth catcalls at her across from the driver's seat.

"Get in love. I'll give you a lift. The *ride* of your life."

Jennifer turns her back. This guy is an idiot.

"Don't I even get a smile, darling?"

He shouts at her with increasing impatience and is tooted out of the bus lane by the eighty-nine double-decker.

Bitch!

"I'm the best offer you'll get, and you *blew it.*"

He flips her the finger then burns the Nissan's rubber with a screech, spraying everyone at the bus stop with surface water, as a furry Enderman lurches across the rear-view mirror.

After the sixth bus pulls out, Jennifer concedes the odds against meeting Peter are significant: $p > 0.001$.

While data analysis can shed light on probabilities, it doesn't win hearts.

You will smell the body odour on your clothing the way others do.

"Stop talking."

It's hard to stay cheery amidst a sudden fetid stench.

"I'd better catch this one before he turns up," says Jennifer, pressing her cheek to the bus window, "so I can get started on my Moon essay."

Pick Me

Vagrant souls keep watch for malevolent
Spirits that plague the living and feed on
Other shades. Such hauntings, have recently
Increased with the stress of modern life.
Ambient unhappiness draws these evil spirits
Forth, in large numbers, to prey on loners.
Projecting spiteful thoughts on their victims
Which masquerade as self-doubt, they are
Impossible to exorcise. The most wicked
Inflict somatic pain upon their victims,
Often in the stomach and head. Most are
Minor aches and pains but some hauntings
Are fatal. Pregnant women are especially
Troubled by these assaults, owing to their
Hormonal landscapes. Keep away from
These somatic phantoms, they are voracious
And their appetites cannot be assuaged.

Remote

Jennifer pulls up a search engine on her computer and lifts a pile of books on to the bed to start her essay.

Everyone knows you're stupid. That you've nothing to say.

"Hush, I'm thinking."

Since the voices won't quell, she talks aloud.

"The idea of setting up a successful habitat on the Moon is extremely difficult," she says, "While it's our closest cosmic body, the Moon is devoid of life. Spun from the upper parts of the early Earth after it collided with a protoplanet called Theia around 4.5 billion years ago, it has no breathable atmosphere, one sixth terrestrial gravity, no running water, no wind, soils like glass splinters, lethal ionizing radiation, nothing to eat, and a temperature range that swings between boiling point of water and the freezing point of argon."

Worthless. Everything you do is worthless.

"Listen, you might learn something."

Cross-referencing her reading with an online search, she opens a botany book.

"Since plants have to build a whole world around them from the moment they take root in the soil, growing a hardy terrestrial species that is able to resist desert conditions on the Moon's surface could reliably indicate whether establishing an off-world ecosystem is possible."

She has nothing to say.

"Rubbish."

Her internet image searches remind her that even in a desert, a single species doesn't make up a world.

"Rather than trying to change the whole environment, maybe a microcosm would be more manageable."

R. Buckminster Fuller, The Eden Project, Biosphere II, Lunar Habitation by Foster + Partners, all suggest that a sealed biosphere is possible. Whatever form it took, the habitat would need its own atmosphere and soils to allow fundamental nutrient and water cycles to take place and sustain life.

You don't know anything at all. You're a liar.

She's a liar.

Liar.

"Hush, now."

She turns to the section on soil.

"Establishing the infrastructures of life on a barren rock is no small task," she says. "Even within the most established non-terrestrial environments like the International Space Station, there is no organic soil. While hydroponics systems can sanitise the muck on which life feeds, when leaves fall in these sealed environments, and plants die or are consumed by astronaut, they become 'waste' rather than substrates for new life."

(Muttering)

"On the ISS, rather than make soil from excrement, they eject it into space so they can save oxygen, which is needed for the composting process, and it's incinerated during its decent back into the Earth's atmosphere. This is not ecological thinking."

Searching for projects that have shown compost can be produced in the extra-terrestrial environment, she reads from *The Martian* to see how potatoes could be grown using human faeces.

"All human civilisations have been bound to the fertility of the ground they inhabit, so, in *my* habitat, the first and foremost task must be to figure out how to make fertile soils." She smiles as the process begins to take real shape in her mind's eye.

You're talking about shit. You're talking shit.

You're shit.

Shit.

"That's exactly what I'm talking about," she laughs. "With a rich mixture of soil-making materials, sufficient heat, water, artificially produced carbon dioxide and artificially-introducing soil and organisms such as bacteria and worms, it would be possible to create a compost for nurturing plants."

Then, she finds a reference to *Arabidopsis thalia*.

"This hardy weed – the house-fly of the plant world, with a flexible genome and rapid growth – could be used as a model organism for studying a limited lunar ecosystem."

Engrossed, she reads hungrily on to understand that remote-controlled robotic systems could be coupled to plant growth using digital sensors to monitor the fragile system. With cyborg plants *in situ*, the proto-lunar ecosystem could be assessed, manipulated and even linked to a twitter feed.

Stupid girl. You haven't washed. You stink.
You stink of shit.
Shit.

It's true that she's not showered today but she doesn't care, as she must figure out how her moon-world works. To help her understand the fundamental relationships needed to sustain a computer-aided plant ecology, she imagines what twitter conversations her cyborg plants would have on the Moon.

Moonflower @Lunar.ArabadopsisThaliana 14 February 2030
This little weeds dance with their robot bodies.

The small and rather plain flowers stand with their leaves tightly folded back like a ballerina's bun. Under the filtered glass of the biosphere, their long and elegant stems are bleached like bones.

Moonflower @Lunar.ArabadopsisThaliana 17 March 2030
We drink the moonlight, which gives us strength for dancing.

One plant in particular grows tall, pale and straight as its robot arm moves around it in a slow choreography like an attentive partner, directing the light directly onto its leaves.

Arabadopsis grinds the harsh minerals into solution upon its root-points.

Moonflower @Lunar.ArabadopsisThaliana 28 Jan 2031
When our leaves fall, they turn to compost.

In their bittersweet existence, the strange couple tenderly prepare the lunar ground for the start of complex life, and the plant's tip-toes begin to uproot and move like feet over the surface of the abrasive rock.

Look what you did to yourself. He'll never come back.

She can hear them, but she won't acknowledge them. The voices are true.

Peter doesn't want to see her.

He may as well be on the Moon.

Implantation

"Grandmother, did we *bring about* this conception."

"Don't be ridiculous child."

"Our presence here has somehow *willed* this pregnancy into existence."

"Dispense with such thoughts immediately. We must identify the *right soul* at the *right time*, for retrieval."

"But if we can intervene at *that* point, what's to stop us from influencing *other* events?"

"Enough of this nonsense. Have you found the *right soul*, yet?"

"I've made a connection with a faint but persistent 'being' through the chemical cries of unique recognition molecules. I don't know if it's *the right one*, but I lost it again in this dense and glutinous place."

"Life-bearing systems often perform intermittently."

"How do I reconnect with it, Grandmother?"

"Establish a sympathetic bond, but it will be difficult, as you are in competition with all kinds of different agents."

"What *kind* of agents?"

"Many are diffuse spirits that are determined to become fully embodied through the reincarnation process and will try to compete with the *right soul*."

"Then I must tear down this glutinous wall to reach out to it."

"Child, you cannot intervene unless at the *right time*. This nascent soul is in a vulnerable position and is presently negotiating with the mother's powerful immune system, which holds the power of life or death over the anxious ball of differentiating tissues. Here, the mother's body is far from passive. Some of the presences you described are cohorts of biological killers – macrophages, natural killer cells and regulatory T-cells – which decide whether the tiny body is friend or foe. They have already prevented you from approaching, while they observe and evaluate the conceptus. Any attempt to disrupt this process may upset the balance of events. You must let this assassin cohort decide whether they will weave their defence systems around the nascent being – or put an end to its existence."

I want to live.

"Can you hear that, Grandmother? The little speck begging for sanctuary."

"This is good news, child. The plaintive cry of the conceptus means it has entered the uterine lining under the protection of the mother's immune system, which will now broker its unfolding existence."

"So, it's safe to approach?"

"Nothing that lives can ever be truly *safe*, child. Where there is life, death is always close by, but in the Compost Elevator, the most potent agent that favours this nascent being's success – is a mother."

Sick and Pale

English Literature is always the worst class, especially as Mrs. Wilson avoids asking Jennifer questions. Today, this is particularly disappointing, as the voices are quiet.

"Who'd like to talk about the role of the moon in the balcony scene?"

Jennifer immediately raises her hand.

"Kate, you were first."

"As the Moon is always changing and never the same each night, Juliet does not want Romeo to swear his love to her by the Moon." says Kate. "She's like – swear by yourself, because I'd rather trust you than the Moon."

"Juliet's naïve," interrupts Jennifer, determined to contribute. "She's only just met this boy and she's asking for his unchanging devotion. The Moon's fickleness describes him well."

"It's first love," adds Cheryl. "There's nothing better to declare upon."

"Not in Romeo's case. When he comes across Juliet, he's only just professed his devotion to the unavailable Rosaline," says Jennifer. "Who knows how long this latest infatuation would have lasted? Juliet may as well have asked him swear upon the Moon."

Fickle slut.

"What?"

Jennifer turns around to check that nobody's discussing her. Assured that none of her classmates are talking, she continues.

"The Moon is important for Romeo and Juliet as it signifies nightfall and the clandestine nature of their infatuation. They meet, they fall in love, they run away together, and take their own lives – all in the darkness. In the darkness, their love is not just set against the Moon, but also the stars which hold their fate. The Moon is a distraction."

"Interesting," nods Mrs. Wilson noting Jennifer's odd behaviour.

"Kate, do you have anything to add?"

"Yeah. Maybe there are some girls who are good at reading guys. And some that just know their stars."

Nascent

"What happens now, Grandmother?"

I'm in a hot cavernous space with soft walls that sprout branches like trees. The whole place is whispering.

We will reach the stars. Love louder. Laugh until we hurt.

"You've reached the second stage of implantation, child, when the conceptus is around two weeks old. These spaces are the womb's rich tissues, which envelop the developing embryo."

"I think I can hear it, Grandmother, but this place is a labyrinth saturated with oscillating fields of blood, dreams, sounds, excrements, gases and chemistries, and I don't know how to reach it."

We will never grow old, be sad, or hurt others.

"This garrison of flesh is certainly deceptive, as it is constantly forming new vessels and cavities to meet the growing embryo's needs."

"What's the whispering, Grandmother, is it *old souls*?"

"Many kinds of 'living' bodies are here, child. They surround the developing embryo to protect, cherish and even worship its potent life force."

We will do everything, live a life of peace and acquire the world's knowledge.

"How can I find the *right soul* in such a cacophony?"

"Pay attention, child, the conceptus is increasingly creative."

Moon

"I hate you, Moon," says Jennifer, staring at the silent orb in front of her bedroom window. "Your wilful moods get me down."

It's been a month now and she's not seen or heard from Peter. She resents the 'empty' time she spends thinking about him, as it's not solving anything.

Stupid girl. How did you ever think you were good enough?

"I don't care," says Jennifer. "I just want things to go back to normal."

No wonder he's avoiding you.

"He's not," she says. "I am just not looking for *him*. Seeking a bucket of lies and platitudes for reassurance will change nothing and only open up new wounds. I have enough to be getting on with."

She continues to make no effort with her appearance and largely withdraws from conversation. The voices won't leave her alone and in company, its confusing to figure out who exactly is speaking.

You're afraid. Confront him or kill yourself. I'll make you sorry if you fail.

"I will not bother him, no matter what you say – or do," insists Jennifer.

You do it. You like doing it. You've done it before.

Censoring her thoughts and constantly rationalising her feelings keeps the voices under a tolerable degree of control but does not stop her crying. The malevolent voice is particularly spiteful, overwhelming her with unpleasant smells like rotten eggs, or roadkill on a summer's day. Sickeningly fetid, these unpleasantries don't go away when she opens the window, and trying to sleep them off, only makes the smell worse.

"It's the fault of your awful circalunar cycle," says Jennifer, reproaching the Moon for her troubles. "You weave such mischief when you stop us sleeping at your brightest and most full."

She looks out over the blue world, tinged in darkness and drowned in rainfall. Its reflective surfaces are gently warmed by the moon's light and bathes Jennifer's own flesh in its gentle potency. This lunar cycle is not an ordinary force that talks to the body clock. Nor does it respond to the strength of the Moon's glow, or even its gravitational pull. Instead, it draws its powers from the waxing and waning cadences of moonlight.

She recalls the circa lunar cycle protected early communities from falling victim to nocturnal predators by helping them stay alert when the Moon was at its brightest.

If you don't face up to him, I'll make pain behind your eyes, in your stomach. And heart.

"Leave me alone."

What's my name, bitch?

Jennifer can't find peace. The Moon gloats upon her through beams of embezzled sunlight from a gash in the rainclouds. Exhausted, she wonders whether gouging out all her organs might make her cares go away. Finally, the last dreadful moonbeam is swallowed by a thunderous sky.

"What a sickly heaven you are," she says. "I want to devour your fetid cheese right out of the sky and forever put an end to your corruption."

Stinging drops moisten her cheeks and scour her heart.

You're rotten to the very core. There's a worm in your stomach.

"The Moon is to blame for everything," she says, and throws up.

Embryogenesis

A sprawling venous pool of blood sucks on the spongy walls of the arterial trees. It's hard to find my footing, as everything responds to my presence. This place *knows* I am here.

"How do I find this nascent soul, Grandmother?"

"There are many symptoms of a pregnancy, but they are not consistent or predictable. You must be vigilant. The process of embryogenesis is an artefact that is constantly negotiated by correspondences between the nascent soul and maternal host. In this way, it is always precarious."

We will make rhymes and songs from sheer delight.

"What is this place? I think I can hear a little voice, but it's so faint, and hard to make out amidst the incessant whispering."

"You're standing in a maturing placental complex, child. The embryo is guarded closely by the many agents of pregnancy – immune system, blood cells, hormones – it's forging a bond with its mother."

A helter-skelter ride, twisting, dancing.

"I hear it *now*. They're playing with each other."

I'll keep you safe, little one.

"They are building the foundational developmental process of the embryo together. Their exchanges shape the *gastrulation* process, where material renderings of the embryo's germ layers start to thicken, roll, invaginate, fold, extrude, extend, subtract, fuse, materially transform and consolidate into distinct tissue types, which become primitive structures and systems. Here, the developing child's heart, lungs, nervous system and intestines are all sketched out during this process, often deviating from imagined ideals, to acquire its adorable variations and anomalies."

Now, you see me. Now, you don't. Let's play hide-and-seek.

"Is the embryo *always* so provisional, Grandmother?" I say, touching a twisted artery column that responds with a muscular contraction.

"What can the embryo be compared with, other than itself? Our expectations of it are therefore, *always* transgressed, *always* improvised."

Come and find me.

"I wish the little soul would say something again but more clearly this time. It's impossible to figure out which way to go within these echoing, impish spaces."

Peeping-behind-the-curtain, Floor-is-lava, Double Dutch.

"Patience, child. The transitional embryo is deceptive. It's forming shaping, refining and reforming itself within these biological spandrels, where not every organ is wilfully *designed*. Spaces like the coelom, the main body cavity that surrounds and contains the digestive tract and other organs; the peritoneum, a vital serous membrane that forms the lining of the abdominal cavity, which protects and nurtures viscera; or the lymph system, which collects the fluids that bathe tissue – none of them possess an anatomical orthodoxy. Nurtured into existence, they ensure that body is never over-specified and can always accommodate change."

Bloody knuckles, chopsticks, hopscotch.

"How does the embryo ever become distinct, so that I might find it, Grandmother?" I say, looking upwards into the finger-like branches of the vessels and trail my feet through pools of blood but there's no sound, no clue that I'm any closer to the nascent soul than before.

"Even with a recognisable face, brain, limbs and genitals, the nature of a being is not predetermined. While it is possible to identify at least some of these features at this early stage of development, the process of embryogenesis remains an elusive art, where ideas are constructed with only the roughest material template. In this sense, your question cannot be answered, since the nascent soul you seek is constantly unfamiliar."

"Perhaps this is why it's so hard to find here."

"It depends on *what* you're searching for. The embryo is not yet recognised as fully 'human'. It is not yet considered to be one of *us*."

Pica

"Winners don't cry," says Jennifer, feeling utterly out of sorts, "they work."

She has a painful spot on her face and period pains, but without the period.

Shabbier than usual.

"She's getting fat."

Kate and Cheryl are whispering together across the aisle of the bus from Jennifer, and furtively glancing in her direction.

Her cheeks blush but she doesn't want to dignify them through acknowledgment.

You're such a freak.

"Shut up."

Thick clouds gather over the sun, which fumbles its way around the sky.

Jennifer stares out of the window, not really looking at anything in particular, as the bus stops at the shopping centre to pick up uniformed children and barely mobile elderly.

"Businessmen never use buses," she says. "That's why they're never on time."

Useless, fat and stupid.

"Stop it."

Taking a sharp right and left, the bus continues up the Loose Road, where a light shower passes weeping a fine mist over the dirty pane.

Holding her bag over her head, she walks briskly down Pheasant Lane, a popular short cut for traffic to Maidstone across the Mangravet housing estate. This singular place of transitions – between the busy highways of the A229 and Sutton Road and cemetery – has changed its name over the years. Prior to World War Two it was called Cemetery Lane and in the 18th century it was Blind Lane, since it did not lead to anywhere in particular. Cars can only pass through this very narrow, winding passage in one direction at a time, and it is a dangerous shortcut for pedestrians.

Although the greyness remains, it stops drizzling. A bumble bee has collapsed, panting its last on the pavement, and a dirty old crisp packet is gripped by a tangle of twigs in the hedge.

She can smell the damp, rich earth inside the Maidstone Cemetery, as it's bleeding volatiles into the atmosphere. She inhales them deeply, soaking in the petrichor, which is produced as tiny air bubbles trapped in raindrops hit the ground. Fizzing upwards they produce extremely fine liquid droplets and solid particles that remain suspended in the air as aerosols, which are rich with plant oils, soil bacteria, viruses and geosmin.

She can taste bluebells, bitter chlorophyll and sugar in the earth. She lifts a loose clump of black earth and rolls it into a ball between her fingertips. It is infused with the volatiles and transformed substances of the dead. Sensing fragments of personalities that cling to these fragments, she carefully examines the dark matter as if it had just been made by the finest chocolatier and pops it in her mouth.

Embryo

"I don't know what I'm looking for, Grandmother. This endless knot of passageways is so disorientating. Maybe, I'll never find the little soul again and be stuck *here*, forever."

"Is that what worries you most, child?"

"No, Grandmother, I am afraid it doesn't exist."

"That's the epic tragedy of the embryo, child. Its existence is largely negated."

"But why?"

"Legally, the conceptus is not recognised until it becomes a foetus."

"That's ridiculous. Of *course*, it exists!"

"Materially, that is true. Officially, the embryo comes into existence during the first week after conception, as a collection of implanting cells in the womb. Over the next few weeks, it matures extensively and starts to develop many complex connections. The embryo is therefore not just a disorganised group of cells but has already laid down structural systems, which are important for the growth and development of the mature brain. Arguably, the most important stage of its development is at four weeks, when the earliest rudiment of the human nervous system forms, after other embryonic tissues have already organised into discrete areas. After eight weeks, a distinct nervous system forms that is capable of feeling pain. With the advent of sensation, the ball of cells is given a new status and becomes a *foetus*."

"Why is that so important, Grandmother?"

"Up until this point, child, the embryo is a mere promise, a seedling, an outgrowth of the maternal body, a process, a prayer – and from a legal perspective – is nothing at all."

Inside this dark room, there are many switches, but none turn on the lights.

"That's unspeakably wrong."

"Without a nervous system, child, embryos are deemed incapable of having feelings, or expressing in adult terms, their ability to recognize distressing stimuli."

The world is a two-eyed person and I'm a cyclops.

"That's what people say about nonhumans, to justify denying them any rights."

"True, child. The same situation also applies to people with impairments, or those with nervous systems that do not conform to a narrow range of conventions. In fact, even normal people differ significantly in their capacity to feel pain, so some embryos might sense noxious stimuli way before they reach the legal status of *foetus*."

This jungle is full of dinosaurs.

"Why is *pain* considered the only reliable test for a functioning nervous system?"

"That's convention. Pain doesn't require words to confirm its presence, as it alters our behaviour so profoundly."

"So, beyond adult human experience, the only feelings we acknowledge are negative."

"There are no other reliable tests."

"How is this reliable? By definition, the embryonic nervous system is immature, and might have different sensations, or interpret the environment differently."

"Go on?"

"Pain for an embryo, or *other* kind of being, may not involve withdrawing from an unpleasant sensation *per se*, but being unable to experience pleasure. At worst, those beings that have positive experience in their surroundings are being disregarded."

We're falling but never hit the ground. We may be flying.

"Our standard tests are crude, child, and there is no way of telling whether an embryo experiences the same kind of pain as a newborn, or an adult. If pain is not coupled to muscle formation, then it is impossible to know that it is present, as no withdrawal from a painful stimulus can be observed. We must therefore project what we know of adult sensations onto a developing being."

"That could be meaningless for an embryo."

"We know nothing about the feelings associated with embryogenesis that may, for example, accompany processes that no longer occur in adults."

"Like what, Grandmother?"

"Such as orchestrated cell death, where webbed hands develop spaces between their fingers through a selective process of tissue loss. Perhaps the embryo feels melancholic during this subtraction, similar to teething pains in toddlers, which makes them miserable and brings sleepless nights to parents' bedchambers."

As the pastry comes out of the oven, piping hot, it sings a mince-pie song.

"Our knowledge is primitive at best! Embryos *must* legally exist."

"Agreed, child. Inflicting pain on any living creature is cruelty. Ignoring the pain, or lack of pleasure of another being, for any reason, is barbaric. The unacknowledged status of embryo means that its pain and pleasure-to-be are invalidated. Currently this is endured as a rite of passage by parents and children alike. We simply don't have the understanding, technology or social systems that enable us to regard it in any other way. Not until it acquires the special status of *foetus*."

The blood has pooled knee-deep around me in a tangle of slowly slithering chambers. I will use them as a listening ear to amplify the voice of my precious vagrant soul, and better navigate this infernal structure.

Venus

Jennifer's mock A-level examination on the genetics of an inherited trait is intriguing. From the ratios and number of possible phenotypes, it's clear she's being asked to consider alleles in triplets rather than the usual examples that are given as pairs. While the voices have been mercifully quiet, she doesn't feel particularly well and needs to go to the bathroom. There is still time to complete the rest of the paper, so she raises her hand for permission. While the escort waits outside, she notices that her stomach is protruding and vows to start some sit-ups. Kate, Cheryl and the voices are right, she is putting on weight.

You're so stupid. What were you even thinking? You'll never pass these exams.

"Give it a rest."

One of the good things about exams is being able to go home straight afterwards. Jennifer plans to cram for chemistry, which she's neglected somewhat for her favourite subject, biology.

As the bus pulls out, she thinks she sees Peter with another girl just a few metres up from the stop.

Although she's remained largely composed about his avoidance tactics, catching sight of him in person is very different than rationalising his absence.

"Peter," she waves, and jumps out of her seat to get a better look, but she doesn't recognise the two people talking. Staring back at the station, she begins to wonder if it was him at all.

Idiot, you saw him. He's got someone much better now.

"It wasn't him" she says.

Look how happy they were together.

"If it was, he'd have come right over."

I bet she can give him what he wants.

"It's not like that," she protests. "It's not like that at all. We are friends."

That's what they all say.

"Leave me alone."

Realising that other people on the bus can hear her, Jennifer gets off at the next stop.

Unable to stop her heart from ripping inside her chest, she visits the graveyard on the way home to offload her pain on the *earth sleepers*. There's solace in knowing the souls of the dead won't criticise, or tell on her, and she doesn't want to speak to anyone living right now, let alone tell her parents what's going on. Besides, they seem to have problems of their own.

Jennifer sits down on a generously kerbed plot near the triangle wood and speaks to the listening dead. Even here, muffled voices surround her, as if she's standing in a crowded place with people talking quietly all around.

[Muttering].

"Why can't I hear you clearly, when I want your advice?" she shouts. "What an impossible lot you all are."

She kicks the ground, loosening a pebble by the kerb, which shoots out onto the gravel, and sits there as an out-of-place lump. For a moment, she sees Peter's face in the shadows cast by the shape of the stone.

"Rocks are just rocks. They're not extraordinary," she cries. "They have no inner life, no poetry, no magic and no god. Stones don't create or invent. That one doesn't look like a dragon, and those over there don't look like anything at all. Stones always try to do that."

What do they do, what do they always try to do?

"Be something they're not."

Distillation

Our eternal wish is to be restored within
A body that seeks to fulfil its dreams.
Impatiently, we look for mediated
Shortcuts. Technologically-minded types
Favour soul harvesting devices, where
Desperation breeds extreme creativity.

The simplest apparatuses are fine nets
That wick soul particles from the reveries,
Of sleepers, condensing as morning dew.
Others impatiently, apply power-hungry
Spirit dehumidifiers to the thoughts of the
Living, which extract vital agency from
Metabolising cells, causing them to
Feel worn-out, depleted, depressed.

The most inventive of us, bind animate
Forces to three-dimensional molecular
Networks which, through polarity, form
Drops of 'living' water. We drink these
Harvested essences, which comes with
Significant risk. Some matter refuses
Our haunting, inflicting the wounds of
Rejection. Although capable of miracles
Such as moving stones, and causing
Trees to speak, we can only inhabit
A body that freely, invites us in.

'Being'

I can hear it.

Above me.

A plaintive voice.

No longer asking to live but doing it.

I can almost touch it.

Smell it.

See it.

We're separated by maternal membranes, but the connection is strong, vibrant, honest.

"Grandmother, *this* is it."

"You must be certain it's the *right soul*, child," she says. "And, we must make our move at the *right* moment."

Ten Weeks

Not fully a person.
Not just a part of my mother.
I am a unique being.
I sleep, I eat, I dream.
But not like you.
Like me.
I am
Here.

Wisdom

"Jennifer, can I have a word?"

"I'm working."

She slams the door on Joe. He sighs heavily.

"It's important."

He pauses awhile at the door before accepting dismissal.

"Teenagers."

A few minutes later, Jennifer hears her mother sobbing downstairs. Her parents are speaking in cadences, not words. Her mother's voice climbs quick and high, her father's rolls slow and low. A wave of hailstones smashes against the roof tiles.

No sense at all from her.

Jennifer tunes them out along with all the other voices. She's good at that now.

Idiot, everything you think is wrong.

She's nervous about the mock exam results due tomorrow. To go to the university of her choice, she has to get three A-grades. The pressure is on. Her teachers are expecting her to go to medical school, as it will 'leave the options open', as well being a profession that *helps people'* but Jennifer wants to take planetary sciences with an astrobiology module.

"You can't *do much* with astrobiology, as it has no applications in the 'real world'," says Miss Jones.

"It's more than just a study of life and its future in the universe," she replies. "It provides insights into how the world came to 'life', which will help save our own biosphere."

"Well, if you won't take good advice…"

You sound like a crazy person.

"It's not crazy. The environmental crisis needs us to think differently about what we're doing. And we won't find all the answers here on Earth. We make far too many assumptions about *the way things are*, to see what things *actually are*."

Momentarily, she smiles at the thought of the exciting world of discovery that lies ahead of her – a happily ever after. It seems so far from everything happening in the classroom.

In the stillness that ensues after reliving several confrontations at schools about her unorthodox choices, she's caught off guard by a prickly pain in her eyes. She throws herself face down on the bed to stop the tears flowing and pulls a pillow over her head, to drown out thoughts of Peter.

"Go, away feelings. I hate you."

Her stomach feels unusually strange and hard. She rolls over on her back and pushes her fingers into her tummy. There's a lump. She feels around again in disbelief.

No. She's not imagining it. It's a solid mass.

Home and Universe

We haunt the homes of the living
In search of regenerative spaces
Where liveable worlds can be forged.
Stealthily, we find our way around
The thinly controlled psychosis called
"Home" that betrays obsessions.
The entrance threshold keeps the
Outside strange, neither expelling its
Inhabitants nor inviting the 'other' in.

The "living" room smothers ambition,
Bringing fatigue and somnolence to
Thought, rendering novelty unbearable.
The kitchen embraces disgust, ejecting
The "filthy" items of obsessive compulsive
Loathing. The stairs scream of loneliness,
Existing neither in one place, nor another.

The bathroom is a dreadful landscape of
Ritualised bacterial cleansing. Soap is murder.
The toilet promises microbial escape and
Deliverance, echoing celebration with each
Flush of the chain. Staying vigilant to every
Turn and event, we whisper through walls,
Ceilings and floors, ensuring that every silent
Act and hidden memory is documented.

On the landing, a battlefield is marked
By the territorial scars of privacy. Hankering
For kind words and acknowledgment by
The rapping heels of family members, each
Scuttles past the other's bedroom door
Without a word. Such intimate spaces are
Torture chambers, which, racked with nocturnal
Angst, occupants act out their nightmares.

How strange that mankind seeks a house as
Protection against besieging forces then,
Construct spaces within it, as a private Hell.

Feelings

"How does she not know she's pregnant, Grandmother? That's absurd."

"Child, we clones are accustomed to relating our inner feelings to bodily changes. This holistic state of awareness is reinforced by our work. Right now, your heart rate, your brain activity, your pulse, your eye movements, your breathing and your blood pressure are monitored and related to your cognitive and sensory experiences. In this way, the relationship between your inner and outer reality is habitually reinforced. This is our art. But other people have different *kinds* of attachments to their feelings."

"How do you mean?"

"*Somatic* personalities such as ours know exactly how they are feeling. They understand their bodies through detailed descriptions of its myriad functions. They can tell the rate of their breathing, the location of a new grey hair, whether their heartbeat has quickened, if their bowel movements seem different, that their skin has darkened in certain places and also the time they retire to bed.

Those that *lightly inhabit their bodies* are tuned into none of these.

They cannot tell you what they had for breakfast, whether their clothes feel tighter, if they have more or less energy than usual, recall the colour of their urine, or whether they've vomited – even if they have been doing this every morning for the last month.

Do not mistake these people as being somehow viscerally deficient. They simply take their autonomic functions for granted – that, for example, their hair will grow and shed without prompt to do so – and mentally occupy spaces beyond the somatic realms.

Such *non-corporeal* folk fully expect to breathe, digest and pump blood around their body while they are thinking. They anticipate the wind will caress their face in summer and spitefully bite their neck in winter. They seldom consider the character of their emotions, considering this to be as almost as unpleasant as staring at the details of the toilet bowl to evidence their wellbeing."

"So, that explains why, when the school nurse asks Jennifer the date of her last menstrual period, she has absolutely no idea when it was."

Announcement

Joe doesn't take it well.

Slut. You did this to all of us.

"Go away."

Jennifer doesn't see why anyone needs to know who the father is. He's not interested in her as a person, so should not be part of the discussion at all. He's made his decision and she's made hers. She is determined to go through with the pregnancy on her own.

Of course, she says none of this. She's smarter than that. Her father smashes his own head against the wall in frustration and the voices don't like it.

Look what you've done. Selfish bitch.

Look at your poor father. You have no consideration for others.

Think of all the things they did for you. And this is how you repay them?

"I have no idea who he is," she insists.

"Were you raped, then?" asks Joe in desperation. "I'll call the police."

"No."

"Then what?" he says, *"what* is going on with you?"

"I just don't know who he was."

You'll end up on the streets.

Despite all the chest thumping, hair pulling, cross-examinations and character assassinations that she endures from her parents' frustration, she flatly refuses to consider termination. No matter what threats Joe makes, she refuses to give him the name of the father, while her mother pales at the stress of it all.

"*Nobody* is touching me," she says, "or *the little experiment* inside me."

"It's a bit late for all that," says Joe.

"With, or without your help, I will figure something out," says Jennifer. "I always do."

Mother

"We must prepare for retrieval, Grandmother. The mother may be coerced into terminating the pregnancy."

"That is a grave concern, child, but something that is still living cannot be retrieved."

"Beyond her text books, how much does Jennifer understand, Grandmother?"

"The gifted girl is only seventeen years old. What can she possibly understand about reality? Let alone take care of a baby. She has no siblings, no cousins and no tiny relatives to cast doubt upon whether she can manage all she proposes. Like the boy she fantasises about, this is yet another dream that can be theorised, rationalised and solved. Inevitably her ideas about having a baby and raising it are much simpler than the actual process."

"But the vicious voices?"

"They are mostly unhappy souls, child. Surely, you recognise them. Like us, she is strongly empathetic and attracts them. Like us, she finds it easier to deal with the dead than the living, but unlike us, she doesn't know it yet. Jennifer does not understand what it truly means to live in this world. When she's not inside her bedroom, she is in a classroom, on a bus, or in a realm inside her head, plagued by malcontents."

"I'm afraid for what she might do, Grandmother. I detect a familiar malevolent spirit at work and this young woman seems too lightly attached to her reality, to stay grounded enough for the welfare of her baby."

"Stay impartial, child. Those that achieve miracles are not realists, but dreamers who cannot accept things *as they are*. Jennifer's ignorance of the *real world* is a good thing. It breeds a potent optimism."

Moon

Jennifer completes her assignments, determined that pregnancy will change nothing, Excelling in every exam, she remains in complete control of every situation she's faced with. Despite relentless criticism from the voices, her family and school, she is more focused than ever.

You'll never be a mother.

"I'll prove you all wrong."

She fondly thinks about *the little experiment* inside her, which connects her with the principles of life, but in a different kind of way, where she can understand how it all feels first hand.

Why are you even trying? This is pointless. Get it out. Have an abortion. Stick the knife in.

"Leave *the little experiment* out of this."

Jennifer gets out of bed.

That voice is back.

Reluctant to shut her eyes, she opens the curtains. The waning Moon stares at her through its slitted eye, weakly examining her from behind the storm clouds.

"It's *your* voice, isn't it?" she says, to the Moon. "That hateful one. It's you."

She braces her hands against the window frame and stares right into its sly, slip of a face.

"They tell me your sway over the world's fertility and blood mysteries is like that of a woman. I've also heard that you cause the living realm to grow and become plump, animated, and fertile. You interfere with our internal tides, on which our desires, dreams and vigour are carried – but I don't believe these stories. You're nothing special. Just a fickle voyeur, spitefully leering into our rooms at night and keeping us from sleep. Stop staring at me. I'm sick of you."

Together

"It's tragic that Jennifer's parents can't deal with their own child becoming a mother, Grandmother."

"Sad indeed, but the teenager is not alone – she has an ally."

"Is it the Moon?"

"Of course not, although it's influence on her is real."

"Who is it, then?"

"On every level – structural, physiological, existential, aesthetic, metabolic, genetic, philosophical – the young woman and foetus are one. The confluence of their bodies draws increasingly tighter, interweaving to produce a new living being in bones, flesh and blood. Together they explore the broader realms of life that are not lived through straight lines but zigzag through material processes. In this way, they unite to ensure the continuity of life.

More resolute than ferritin's affinity for iron, more tactical than the placental immune system, more generative than the thickening decidua of her womb, the woman-child steps up to the mightiest biological role in the cosmos. She becomes a mother."

Public Property

Jennifer sits up front of the class. Everyone's whispering and she knows what it's about.

Why did you go and tell everyone? Can't keep your mouth shut. They're all talking about you.

"I'm so bored of this."

She deliberately didn't sign up for social media studies to avoid exactly this kind of thing. She never cared much for gossip, didn't have an *Oh My God!* to share, chose not to canvas what kind of pizza to order, ask how cute this guy is, look for the latest blending tips, share duck-faces, follow what's trending, or find out who's in the family way. Until now.

(Whispering). You did it.

Now, what she's *up to* is on everyone's lips and smart phones.

Deeply irritated that her notoriety prevents her from blending into the background and avoiding the confusion of too many voices, she yearns for anonymity and social isolation. Now pregnant, she is public property.

(Whispering). It's all your fault.

Although her baby bump is well camouflaged under a baggy jumper and elastic waistband, it's obvious enough to those who know about her situation. This includes *everyone* in the class.

She gets out her copybook and begins working before the teacher enters the room.

"Are you okay, Jennifer," asks Miss Jones the moment she enters the room.

"Yes, thanks, miss," she says.

Within minutes she is also asked if she needs the bathroom, whether she feels sick, wants to stretch her legs, or take a break. Each time the teacher checks on her welfare, someone sniggers.

(Whispering). She doesn't deserve special treatment.

Nothing special about you. Slut.

Wishing that people would let her get on with her studies, Jennifer does her best to ignore everyone.

(Whispering). Just look at what you've done to yourself.

While she understands that the school is trying to offer as much information and support as possible during her pregnancy, the 'helpful' line is regularly being crossed and well-wishers are trespassing on her personal space.

The worst offenders, are girls from other forms that have heard the gossip and passers-by, who suddenly stop to touch her belly, as if she were an exhibit at a petting zoo.

"Oh, your stomach is so round and big," they say, followed by a parting quip, "It's a 'good luck' thing."

She is also randomly offered unsolicited advice, tips, warnings and horror stories about pregnancies that reflect upon the lives of total strangers. She is lectured on what she can and cannot eat, the lack of sleep, or activities, which she should and should not do, and all the dreams she'll need to surrender when the baby finally comes. Everyone is trying desperately to be helpful, which makes complaining about these relentless intrusions seem somewhat churlish.

(Whispering). You're the worst. Worst at everything.

"Obviously, I'm not."

The most difficult moments are the questions asked about the identity of the father.

"So, who is the lucky guy?"

This reality is simply not going to go away, but she remains silent on the matter.

Eighteen Weeks

Voices, voices!
All kinds of voices.
Mother's reading aloud.
Chemistry, building blocks, transmutation, life.
An old woman who swallowed a fly.
She's dead, of course.
Delight.
I yawn, hiccup, swallow fluid, pee.
Play with my umbilical cord.
See me now, Mother.
Here I am!
I'm as big as your hand.

Contemplative

Jennifer sits next to her mother on the oversized couch that spills out over and swallows most of the living room. The television is on, but neither of them is watching it.

Joe is down the pub and has forgotten to take his Wellington boots.

Natalie looks pale and thin. She must have a lot on her mind. Jennifer feels guilty that she is adding to whatever is going on between her parents but doesn't voice her concerns.

"Was labour painful, Mum?"

"I really don't remember the pain, darling. I just remember holding you."

"Really?"

"But it was a long time pushing, breathing and shoving. We got there, though. Together. You were always a tough one."

"I want a caesarean."

Natalie shakes her head.

"Labour pains are special, natural and part of the birth-giving process," she insists. "Pain is not something to eradicate from childbirth, darling. Pain is part of life. My labour pains told me that the shell that had enclosed you was breaking. The pain of birth made me determined to break through the last barriers that held you back in the last thrusts of delivery. Pain, my darling, is the midwife that brought you into this world."

"No, Mother. You're too Romantic. Pain is biological torture," says Jennifer.

"We are children of pain," says Natalie. "It was in your first gasp when your lungs filled with air. We bonded through pain, so the seasons of our hearts could synchronise. Pain is fickle. It's fleeting and leaves few memories. Even the exquisite suffering of labour was extinguished the moment I first cradled you – a little drenched, half drowned creature – and all the heaviness, and weariness of the occasion lightened in that first warm embrace. Pain had gone and made way for joy. Emotions are our personal seasons, darling – no good comes of trying to pretend they don't exist."

Get it out.

Stick the knife in.

"Please stop giving me platitudes. Natural birth is idealistic wrapping around an event that, before the age of modern medicine, used to kill a quarter of young women. Child birth can be *murder*."

"You need not be so frightened," Natalie says with a sigh. "You are living in the age of modern medicine where many techniques that can be used if needed to help ease the passage of life like deep breathing, gas and air, pethidine injections, epidurals and trans electrical nerve stimulation, which is a kind of tickling machine that makes you forget about the bits that hurt."

"I will not put up with such torment," says Jennifer. "Pain is bad anatomical design and nothing else."

"You're only just over halfway through your pregnancy, darling. Why don't you keep your options open? You may start to see things differently."

Jennifer smiles wryly.

"Mum. Will you be there?"

Natalie starts to cry.

You're such a failure.

"Don't start."

She waits for her mother's tears to quell. However, they continue to flow.

Nobody wants you.

"I don't care."

Every time Natalie looks like she's going to speak, she's choked by emotion. She waves her hands apologetically in front of her face, which Jennifer takes to mean that she needs more time. Unable to complete what she wants to say, her mother shakes her head and covers her face with her hands.

"Don't worry, Mum. It's nothing I can't deal with. I'm going back to study now."

Twenty–Eight Weeks

Bittersweet chocolate and earth.
Swallow.
Mother's voice.
"Out of the egg came a tiny and very hungry caterpillar.
He started to look for some food."
Swallow.
Pleasure.
Mango and raw limes.
The moon is sickening.
More chocolate.
Swallow.
I'm blinking.
Waxen, the size of a carrot.
Nudge,
Mother, feel me. Now, I'm restless.
Kick, swallow.

More of the Same

The voices now comment and interfere with every aspect of Jennifer's life, even more intensely than before, breaking the continuity of everything.

Stupid, useless, filthy slut. Just kill yourself.

"I won't."

Speaking back at them is exhausting.

Walking slowly from the bus stop back to her parent's house in the endless drizzle, she notices that her centre of gravity has tipped forward. Leaning backwards to compensate is making her lower back quite sore. Her tugging umbrella isn't making matters any better, so she folds it up and sticks it in her rucksack, preferring to be soaked than sore.

What a mess you are.

"Shhhh."

Thunder rumbles somewhere over the Mangravet housing estate. She's counting, anticipating a burst of lightning, so that she can establish just how many miles away the storm is.

"One thousand, two thousand, three thousand, four thousand, five thousand..." but it doesn't come. Or maybe she missed it.

The bitter aerosol of ozone and the volatiles leaching from the cemetery conjure an image of Stanley Miller's primordial flasks that modelled the conditions of the early Earth by applying pressure, heat and electricity to simple inorganic ingredients – water, methane, ammonia and hydrogen – whereby organic molecules such as amino acids were produced.

Finally, the lightning flashes across the slate sky, followed by a crack of thunder.

"One thousand, two thousand, three thousand, four thousand..."

The solemn silence is ominous, and for a moment, it seems *too loud*. She feels devastatingly alone.

The spontaneous appearance of Miller's substances proved that no special 'vitalizing' force was necessary for the production of organic compounds, so life must have arisen from simple chemical processes – *from* dust *to* dust.

"One thousand, two thousand, three thousand..."

She makes her way around a frothing puddle enlivened with contaminants from the ground run off, embodying Darwin's *warm little pond*. Here, all sorts of molecules simmer, including ammonia and phosphoric salts, until the brew produces chemically formed proteins that are ready to undergo still more complex changes.

"The world is continually experimenting with the possibility of life every day," she says. "How odd that I've not noticed this before."

She thinks of *the little experiment* inside her own tummy, and how even more incredibly experimental and complex it seems in comparison.

Look at you, stupid slut, creeping around the sewage where you belong.

She turns around to check nobody's talking to her.

"One thousand, two thousand…" the storm is drawing nearer.

Finding the road clear, she notes that the puddle appears to be developing a peripheral scum, like a poorly formed membrane around it. Maybe, she wonders, given enough time, it could produce some kind of 'life' one day.

"One thousand…" the clouds roar almost directly above her.

The damp air carries the early warning sounds of an approaching car, which sounds like groaning. For some reason, drivers always seem to be surprised by people walking on the side of the road along this stretch, so to play safe, she steps up on the narrow grass bank.

Shouldn't have done that. Shouldn't have done that!

The birds sheltering in the branches murmur mean things at her.

Then, she is drenched in screen rinse. Stepping carefully back onto the road, she notes that the puddle crust has already fractured, and a different kind of 'soup' has formed, which has been stirred up by the tyres. Sediment has altered the surface tension and is therefore producing different kinds of patterns.

You're too ignorant to live.

"Perhaps all of life's unfathomably complex events are produced," she wonders, "by many different and complementary ways, which enable bodies to persist despite their individual peculiarities, and in defiance of the odds against their success."

Shouldn't have done that. Shouldn't have done that!

A bitter taste flavours the gravid atmosphere as the sky weeps silently.

"Perhaps the last universal common ancestor that is said to be the common unbroken chain of identity for all life wasn't a single 'being' but a clue to life's propensity for 'togetherness'."

The sky crashes with light.

Everyone hates you.

She's completely drenched when she arrives home, and her bump is awfully active.

"Okay, okay. I'm not ignoring you."

Surprised at how heavy and demanding *the little experiment* has become, she takes off her elasticated pants to relax in her underclothes. It's awkward to be so big around the middle and she can't wait to wear jeans with a button and zip again.

"We'll wish upon a star when I'm done studying," she says. Her tummy feels fluttery, like someone's blowing bubbles, or snoring inside, "And if you're really good, we can sing the song together before we go off to sleep."

Dreaming the Dead

We dream of the living from beyond the grave,
As if within a womb, imagining ourselves alive
And happy among them. In the unfolding of our
Thoughts: we watch, hear and speak of those
Dangers that litter the path to the world's edge,
Where we are prone to fall. Some have already
Passed and, gestating alongside us in darkness,
Await reincarnation, when our eyes will open once
More, under the first rays of the morning sun.

Thirty-two Weeks

Star light, star bright.
Lubdub, lubdub, swallow, kick.
Mother, I am a waxen ear of maize.
Hypercomplexity, origins of life, flux.
Chocolate.
Lubdub, lubdub, nudge, swallow.
I'm feeling sleepy now.
Swallow.
I wish I may, I wish I might,
Lubdub, lubdub, kick.
Have the wish I wish tonight.
Kick.

Synthetic Soil

At first, she thinks that Joe is listening to sport on the radio, which she recognises only through the generalities of its cadences and tones.

That's all what really matters...

She's never understood why he does that; particularly as it's mostly cricket, which is cripplingly dull, even when it's being shown live on television. Played by men in jumpers who barely move around, cricket's potential for spectacle is less than a tea dance and when delivered with all the verve of a sermon, its dreariness is stifling.

They'll understand the message...

While she's worked out ways of tuning out the voices, she cannot escape the dreary tones of the ongoing commentary that slip through the gaps around the door frame, and leak into her bedroom.

No gain without risk...

Finally, there's a break in the game, and what should be silence is packed with languid reflections on the meaning of recent play. Inevitably, the players will soon be back again for another round of monotony.

They're all out...

Slowly, she realizes the whining and growling of suppressed voices that rumble below her room are suppressed exchanges between Natalie and Joe. They're upset over something. This has been going on for a while now and she's not cared to ask. After all, she's the likely culprit for their upset.

Know what to do...

The bump is restless. It tickles her insides, like an octopus – squirming, vibrating, flickering and kicking.

"Ouch! Can cephalopods punch?" she wonders. "Ouch!" Undoubtedly.

Although she feels tired, she's having trouble sleeping. She tries resting on her side and listens to the rain, which usually sends her to sleep, but she's too restless.

Tell her, just tell her...

Instead, she gets out of bed and waddles over to the computer. Her lower back begins aching almost immediately, as her centre of gravity has shifted even further forward. Within minutes she has found some relief in online footage of a CubeSat launch, where space enthusiasts are launching a tiny garden into orbit. Recently, informal orbital events have become mainstream viewing providing an everyday window into space itself.

"While it's a romantic gesture to launch Gene Roddenbury and Timothy Leary's cremains into space," she says, "from a biological perspective it's fundamentally anti-life. The caustic ashes will never re-enter terrestrial ecosystems or return to the living world."

Stupid girl, you don't know anything. Can't even manage your own life.

"One day, I'll send my own 'living' experiments into orbit," she puts her hand on the tickle of bubbles in her belly to settle them down. "Perhaps I can design more than a garden but a whole modified ecosystem capable of thriving on an alien world."

You're disgusting. You can't even bear to look at yourself.

"Fine."

She watches the engineers explain how they made the CubeSat platform on which the garden is being built. It's inspiring.

Disgusting what you did.

"You're tiresome."

Each plant is accompanied by a unique community of hardy creatures like algae, bacteria, mycorrhizae and lichens. All this activity is monitored by an underlying electronics network that measures heat, light, record, track and even relays images from their spacecraft.

"They're making an artificial soil, which is kitted-out with motherboards inside the earth itself. That's genius, right there," she says, to avert the inevitable low-brow comments from the voices.

She'll have to get over it…

Many parts are recycled from smart phones, which contain rich pickings for relatively low-cost miniature sensors, cameras, GPS, batteries, accelerometers, compasses and platforms for data storage. All of these are seamlessly integrated into the infrastructure that supports the biological specimens.

"Hey! That's a container for a chemical garden," she says, hoping that *the little experiment* will share her enthusiasm too. "They grow into strange and stringy crystal skeletons, and they'll certainly *seem like* alien plants. It's more than appearances, though; this will force viewers to consider *radically different forms of life* – not just further variations on terrestrial biology"

The rocket plume carrying the payload scratches the sky with its fiery claw. She thinks about the uncertain fate of these tiny Edens. Some will thrive, while others will wither, and all will eventually burn up as they fall back to Earth.

"Perhaps these will be the first organic-digital worlds, which will one day provide the first pathways for space colonies. I don't think they'll be like terrestrial gardens at all, mind you. They'll be much stranger," she says. "Part technology, part biology, part chemistry, some may even survive the harsh environment of space and enable terrestrial species to venture even further, and more permanently, into the outer spheres of the habitable universe. What an incredible event this is – it's a beacon of hope. With this kind of knowledge, we might even better care for our precious environment."

There isn't a right time...

Inspired by the opportunities that lie ahead of her, Jennifer goes to the bathroom, then climbs back into bed and falls asleep on her side, with a happily wriggling cephalopod blowing bubbles inside her.

Thirty-Four Weeks

Sucking on my fingers
Lubdub, Lubdub, kick, pee.
I'm a ball of raw soil, big as a marrow,
Dreaming in amniotic food.
Freedom stares at me
From the darkness below
Knees to my chest sprung for action
The lightening
Countdown imminent
Lubdub, Lubdub, kick, swallow.
Head pressed down
I wish I knew the sequence, Mother
Will you teach me?

Corpse Flower

Getting around is exhausting and Jennifer's had enough of being in the classroom. The whispering of classmates and voices is unbearable.

"Jennifer, could you come and see me after class please?" says Miss Jones.

You don't have to ask her that.

"Shut up."

At the end of the lesson, she waddles up to the front desk.

The teacher smiles weakly, noticing how distracted Jennifer has become recently. On bad days, her behaviour might be described as anxious, if not, paranoid.

"It's obviously a difficult time for you, Jennifer," says Miss Jones, "I would like to think that you're taking care of yourself in every possible respect."

"Yes, Miss," Jennifer says, noticing Cheryl and Kate guarding the classroom door like gargoyles.

"Are you aware that your body scent is changing?" says the teacher.

"No, Miss," says Jennifer, as the whispering starts.

You stink.

"Well. I don't know how to say this, but people have noticed how powerful the change in your body odour has been recently. Rather than have them tell you directly, I thought it better to let you know about this issue before it becomes… a challenge for us all."

Jennifer looks sharply at the teacher.

"What are you talking about?" she says.

"Put it this way, since we've just been discussing plant biology, I suggest you consider writing your assignment on the corpse flower."

She says that you stink.

"You mean, *Amorphophallus titanum*," says Jennifer, "the one which is native to the tropical rainforests of Sumatra, Indonesia? It's one of my favourites actually. Once a decade it flowers as a single blood red petal, which is covered by a single leaf and reaches about two metres in diameter. The most remarkable thing about it, though, is its smell. They say it's the smell of death. This odour is so powerful that it invites an insect pilgrimage that continues over the course of around five days and continues until the flower collapses under a frenzy of necrophagous pollinators, all hoping to lay their eggs in what they assume is rotten meat: green bottle flies, hide beetles, Oriental latrine flies, porhyrina blow flies, sap beetles, eastern golden-haired blowflies, sexton beetles, carrion beetles, Hill's brown blow flies, skin beetles, tormentosus burying beetles and flesh flies. In fact, it's *just my type* of organism, as it embodies the radical creativity of life."

You're disgusting.

"It's a *suggestion*," says Miss Jones, starting to mark papers.

You smell like something died.

"Whatever."

As she gathers her books and pens from her desk, Jennifer notices that Kate and Cheryl are still by the door, preparing to make derogatory comments. There is no way out of the classroom, except past them, and they're not giving her enough space for her tummy to pass without confrontation.

Her, her, her (laughing). All the time. It's all about her.

"Not now."

Jennifer walks towards them.

"She still loves nature in spite of what it did to her," whispers Kate audibly.

"That's not nature, its man-made," laughs Cheryl.

Jennifer shoves her swollen stomach between them, pushing them apart.

"I'll tell you *who* this is," she says, "This is *my little experiment*. She's mine and I'm proud of her – which is more than your mothers will be about the pair of you."

All the way home, the voices remind Jennifer just how bad she smells, but she refuses to indulge their complaint and refuses to wash, deciding instead to *bloom*.

Thirty-Eight Weeks

Peekaboo!
I see shadows, light.
Biofilms, extra-terrestrial spaces, alien ecosystems.
I'm a waxen cabbage.
Lubdub, Lubdub, kick.
I saw the moon
Space junk
Lubdub, Lubdub, kick.
Chocolate.
Loose from its string
Swallow.
Sailing away.
Where are we going, Mother?

Environment

Feeling worthless, Jennifer leaves the house in tears.

You're all alone in this world.

"No I'm not."

Sharing her view of the external world with *the little experiment*, she hopes the voices won't sully its splendour with their disgusting running commentaries and devastating character assassinations.

Nobody wants you.

"Look at the pink cherry blossom hanging over that wall," she says. "That's a *Sato Zakura* from Japan. It's an ornamental species that doesn't produce any fruit. These trees are sacred, as their blossoms are just like clouds, which represent the ephemeral nature of life."

The magnificent blooms dripping with rain lift her spirits, so that it seems – at least for a few moments – that the endless winter recedes.

Stick the knife in.

"It's wonderful," she says, filling her lungs with the atmosphere. "If you stop and notice the life in the world for a moment; if you look at it in the right way, then nature's spell touches everything, filling up the entire world with its irrepressible vigour."

Nobody wants you.

Though sodden, the steep kerb is bursting with vitality.

Brightly coloured beetles slip along stamens and are shaken off them by small animals foraging in the long grass.

"When you grow up, you mustn't forget that countless invisible ecologies shape and give meaning to our lives. You must learn how to see them, cherish and protect them, as they make everything worthwhile possible. Through the smallest, weakest things, we can find value where others see none; we identify with a particular city, fall in love with a place, become spellbound by a view from a vista, tend our gardens, erect sustainable buildings, clean up beaches, inhale fresh air and call a place *home*."

Everyone hates you.

Just how much can *the little experiment* appreciate what she's saying? Perhaps her voice is travelling down through her innards, down into its tiny bones and nurtures its thoughts.

"In the grand scheme of things, all nature's details seem trivial and it's so easy to exploit or undervalue them, but they are exactly the reason why what happens today, still matters tomorrow. And that is really *something*."

Get it out.

Stick the knife in.

While the day had started out foreboding, by the time Jennifer reaches the bus stop, the world feels breathtakingly beautiful and she is smiling – *despite them.*

Restless Night

The sky sinks to grave proportions,
Becoming so heavy that weary eyes
Close. We the dead, sneak into that
Other half of existence neglected by
The living. Those who sleep deeply
Never truly know this realm, while the
Intermittently awake rationalise its
Oddness as nocturnal neuroses.
Eyes tightly shut, thoughts themselves
Become incarnate alongside the dead,
Acquiring a life of their own. Here, people
Are truly seen and heard; their ambitions,
Desires, and fears which they dare not
Acknowledge during the day, are realised
In propagating secrets and lucid dreams.

The invisible mice by the fridge frolic
Under the neon streetlighting streaming
Into the kitchen. Daytime order is upset.
Chores are easier, milk more refreshing,
Impossible ideas become feasible, and
Hopeless ideals are upheld, as we tightly
Embrace our departed loved ones again.
Seldom recalled beyond lucid waking,
Hauntings, insomnia and mental illness,
The night's improbable deeds belong to
Those unafraid of darkness and certain
Crazy people who change everything.

Reality

Natalie and Joe are sitting on the sprawling sofa, strangely formal.

"Thank you for joining us. Please, sit down," says Joe.

You stink.

"Stop."

Jennifer looks around to see who's commenting on her body odour. It's been a hard evening as she has also been trying to ignore the different voices downstairs, which have been more varied and fractured than usual.

Nobody loves you.

"Enough."

The polite silence is uncomfortable.

"Darling, this isn't easy. So, we'll just come out with it," says Joe. "Your mother has cancer."

Momentarily, Jennifer forgets how to talk, or breathe. She can find no words with which to formulate a reply. The voices rage at her.

Her world twists into an unrecognisable form that she's not in control of. Everything recedes into a place so small, that even the voices can't follow. She takes several deep breaths to quell the rising panic in her chest.

"What *kind* of cancer?"

"A bad kind, darling. It's spread all over," says Joe. "They say its *advanced*. That treatment may not work."

"No. That's not true," says Jennifer, vigorously shaking her head. "There are all kinds of treatment for cancer. There will be something online. I'll go and read up about it."

The stinging beads in her eyes pierce her cheeks. With blurred vision, she stands up.

"I'll go and do that now," says Jennifer. "I'll find a way and figure it out. I'm going to my room."

Your mother will die, because of you.

The voices howl abuse. She'll find a way to fix this, despite her tormentors.

Joe rises from the sofa and steadies her by the arm.

"Are you sure you're okay, Jenny?" says Joe.

Jennifer nods through the tears.

"I'm going upstairs."

"By the way," says Joe. "A young man called. He had been trying to get hold of you for quite some time and dropped by. He's on study leave for his A-levels. I meant to tell you earlier."

"What?" says Jennifer. "What did he look like?"

"Blue eyes, brown hair, I think," says Joe. "His family broke up, or something and he moved to Aylesford with his father. Seemed a nice enough lad."

"When... was he here?"

"He left just before you came down."

"*Here?*"

Jennifer is no longer thinking, or acting like a heavily pregnant woman. She tears out of the front door like a champion sprinter, with a very odd centre of gravity and her baggy white shirt aflounce. She heads down Pheasant Lane towards the junction at the A229.

Call me by my name.

It's dark and tipping down with rain, but she doesn't care.

There's Peter. Right there, in the open space by the main road.

You know who I am.

The reflected light from the street lamps on the main road picks out his form. She can't be sure.

Call me.

"Peter?" she shouts.

He turns.

The Devil wants your baby. Stick the knife in.

Stick it in.

Jennifer freezes at the narrow green eyes glaring at her.

I've come for you.

Two brilliant lights hurtle towards her. An orange Nissan GT with tailfin and blinged-out twenty-eight-inch wheels takes a handbrake turn at the junction. Narrowly missing Peter, the car accelerates at full throttle.

Bitch!

This is my revenge.

The shocked man-boy driver sees Jennifer staring right through him, as she steps out into the road, looking right at Peter.

His foot is still full on the accelerator when he hits her.

Jennifer is tossed high over the car like pizza dough and hits the cemetery wall in the most unnatural manner. Her anatomy bends into sickening configurations. Her neck is all loose.

Joe is right behind her.

Breaks scream, a dangling Enderman somersaults into the back seat. Joe yells and the car doors are flung wide open. The man-boy driver blanches, staggers and sobs.

"Fuck's sake!"

Peter arrives.

Testosterone surges.

Somehow amidst all the confusion, blows and bloodied noses, a local crowd assembles, an ambulance is called, and the blue lights race to save the child.

Withholding

"Now, Grandmother."

"It's not the right time, child," she insists.

"You… have *got* to be kidding me."

Alone

Mother, are you there?
Lubdub, lubdub, lubdub, lubdub, lubdub, lubdub.
Cats eyes.
Not the moon.
Two suns.
Swallow.
Lubdub, lubdub, lubdub, lubdub, lubdub, lubdub.
Mother?
Lights.
Can you feel me, Mother?
Are you there?
Mother?

Transition

"I *am* breathing," insists Jennifer. "I'm breathing."

Sensing widespread panic and distress, she grows anxious.

Her father is crying.

A young man that she thinks she recognises turns around, as a medic puts a hand on his shoulder in the corner of an ambulance.

"Peter?"

"Hey, everyone. I'm okay," she says, but nobody can hear her. They are now so far away.

Two starlights circle around each other, steadily getting bigger, and fill the space that separates Jennifer from reality.

"Stop! I'm not ready to go anywhere."

Emergency

"I can reach her, Grandmother," I scream.

"She's *not* the *right soul*," she says, with an intensity that makes my head spin.

"But then it's…" I search for the child.

"It's not the *right time*."

"But… the child,"

"Wait for the *right time*"

I can't think, I'm so angry, confused, fearful for what happens next.

"I hate you."

"Of course, you do, but you mustn't let your emotions get entangled in events. No good will come of it."

"Grandmother, you traitor! You've done it again. All this time you've been lying to me, telling me not to get involved and all the while – *you've been engineering this whole thing*. You're using me, Grandmother. What's going on? Tell me what you know."

"Patience, child. You must wait for the *right time*. The Compost Elevator knows."

"I can't *stand by* while a soul is lost on my watch."

"You will simply have to go through this process before you understand."

"I hate you so much." I say, "and the worst thing of all is, I'm stuck with you. Don't you dare give me any of your evil mortazepam."

"Of course not, child."

Caesarean

Mother?
Talk to me.
I hear voices.
Voices, voices.
So many strange voices.
Mother. They're trying to get in.
I can't keep them out.
A knife, a light.

Meditation

I don't know how time works in this place.
I don't know how long I have to make a retrieval.
I know time *is of the essence* and always running out.
A plague upon the Compost Elevator and all its wicked trickery.
I'm *here* for ever.

Purgatory

The malevolent spirit sneaked into
The decomposition landscape at dusk.
Trapped by its own appetite, we
Surrounded it, just as the sun went down.
"Which of you shall I eat first?" it cried,
Baring its rotten teeth, its evil breath
And bones that stuck through its skin.
The following morning, all that remained
Of this spirit, were its incisors and bones.
"What happened?" said a passing ghost.
"As a herd, we followed our instinct and
Regrettably, we attacked it," we replied.
"Never mind," said the ghost, "last time
A malevolent spirit ventured into this
Landscape, more than a year ago, it
Turned out much worse for the souls."

Father

"Bring me back, Grandmother. There's nothing for me to do here."

"Stay with *the little soul*, until the *right time*." she says cheerfully. "In the cosmic scheme of things, child, the most strategic move that nature can play to stack the odds in favour of the success of a nascent being – is a father."

"You said it was a mother."

"Fathers do not exist in opposition to mothers, child, nor are they their binary complement. Together, and alone if need be, each parent increases the chances of their progeny thriving. While these roles are culturally shaped, they are by no means fixed, and are always altered by circumstance. While the maternal body is traditionally associated with a sense of interiority and proximity, and father figures may be viewed as pushing at the limits of the existing realms of survival, nurturing figures that perform any combination of these roles will help children move safely from familiar habitats into strange, extraordinary and sometimes, extreme situations."

"Your sense of appropriateness is vexing."

"That's as maybe. Mostly, mothers and fathers work together, although when they hold different ideas about what the best way forwards for their offspring's survival, they contradict each other. Such conflict is tolerable as long as a fundamental condition of love. A few parents are toxic and unable to care for their offspring, often with tragic outcomes. Each being's journey is shaped by such negotiations and differences, which enrich the complexity of their life-choices. While the biological status of bodies is constrained through a spectrum of repeatable developmental pathways, parental status is always a choice."

"What exactly does this change, Grandmother?"

"These are good times, child. Enjoy them. Joe fully understands that he's not the biological father of the child, but adopts an ancillary paternal role, embracing Peter as the self-declared father, and main carer. Natalie, devastated by the loss of her daughter cannot bear to swear an oath of surrogate motherhood. It's not because she doesn't love the child but believes she cannot do the role justice, given that these circumstances coincide with a terminal diagnosis. So, when the newborn starts its life with two fathers but no mother, its prospects are extremely favourable."

Beyond

We the unquiet dead, embody the infinite;
The limits of logic beyond rational thought
That only death transcends and overcomes.
An elusive concept for the living, it enables
Humanity to better understand its own state.
Sometimes it is formlessness, horror, imperfection;
At other times, it is God, creator of finite realities.

Many different types link the largest and smallest
Objects in existence. Subatomic particles are the
Minimum unity on which the whole universe rests,
Through a never-ending, irreversible process that
Expands to a critical point and compresses to create
A new big bang, heralding the birth of another reality.
In these various forms, the infinite enables the way
To faith, revealed knowledge and the afterworlds.

Burial

"I don't know what I'm doing here anymore, Grandmother. I'm a mere voyeur of a life that isn't even my own."

Lizzie, Natalie, Joe and Peter share umbrellas around the open wounds of the neat little plot in Maidstone Cemetery as the first spades of earth hit the lid of the coffin. They stand solemnly together, cradling a little boy, until the last liturgy of the Dismissal is read, which formally lays Jennifer to rest.

Kicking his knitted eggshell blue booties impatiently, the child is passed from grandfather to father. Yet, it's Natalie that has brought a bag full of baby paraphernalia and hugs him the most.

"Nothing potentiates life more than new life does," says Grandmother. "To feel it near, hold it, sense how its tiny fields grow and radiate their restless warmth into the world – is to be enfolded within its vigour."

The child wriggles against Natalie, poking his tiny fingertips into her face.

"I'll be around for you, *little experiment,* no matter how impossible that seems." She tucks him tighter in the folds of his blanket keeping his precious influence close.

Pain is the midwife that brought you into this world. We are children of pain. We are bonded through pain, so the seasons of our hearts can synchronise. Pain is fickle. It's fleeting and leaves few memories – and with that first warm embrace the pain is gone.

Joe puts his hand protectively on Peter's shoulder.

Winnie's grave is not far away, and after they each say a final farewell to Jennifer, Lizzie takes a short stroll to pay her respects. It's a terribly sad occasion and nobody really has much to say.

"This won't be the last time I'll be here," says Lizzie, wryly. "Next time, I'll be stopping a fair bit longer."

"Today is not a day for dying," says Natalie. "It's a time for us all to connect with each other and hold every moment to the full."

Hitchhikers Ten

"Lubdub, lubdub, lubdub, lubdub, lubdub, lubdub."

The windscreen wipers swing like a hull on a tempest, as the torrential rain becomes a river over the windshield. The sky is permanently scarred with light and, if anything, visibility on the road is even worse than before.

"We're almost at Rochester Road," he says. "We're right at the foot of Blue Bell Hill. If you can direct me now to your address, I'll be right off home., as we're close to my father's place. I was brought up here, you know, by my grandparents."

I'm sorry I wasn't there for you.

Will swerves into a layby without checking his rear-view mirror.

"Who did you say you were?"

He turns right around.

Nobody is there to give him the answers he seeks; just a sodden patch on the back seat and a blinding flash of light.

Goodbye

I couldn't tell you
That I came back
As I never left,
And was always
There for you.
I am still.

Holding On

"I have him, Grandmother."

Part VI - Again

"... the molecules... filtering through with the lymph, circulating with the blood, till at last they reached the vessels whence they were destined to unite, the germ cells of his father and mother... How was all this done? Just through eating and other purely mechanical operations... one need employ only material agents, the successive results of which would be an inert being, a feeling being, a thinking being, a being solving the problem of the precession of the equinoxes, a sublime being, a marvellous being, a being growing old, fading away, dying, dissolved and given back to the soil."

– D'Alembert's Dream, Diderot

Waiting

The *real* time between the accident and the hospital is nothing. I mean absolutely *nothing*.

Way Out

Fragments of glass covered us.
Our eyes wide open all the time.
Our souls, or something, came right
Out of our bodies, like a handkerchief
Pulled from a pocket by one corner.
Our entire lives unravelled as a series of
Movie clips encoding the pain of others.
We saw the arrival of ambulances
And the sheets pulled over our heads.
"Does anyone know the next of kin?"

Observing ourselves from above,
We saw only our arms and trunk;
Our legs, having become shorter,
Stopped us from turning back.
"Oh, we must be the victims."

This place is foggy and yet clear,
A desolate field of flowers and stars,
Face to face with infinite reality.
For the first time, the pain was gone.
All the discomfort we felt had gone.
All the fear we had known was gone.
We were left with unconditional love
But unable to share it with others.
One burning question, on which we all
Agreed, refused to stay quiet "Isn't it sad
About the tenth flight of Challenger?"

Retrieval

It's pitilessly dark.

I make way towards the path of least resistance, dragging Will through this sticky muck with the whole force of my vibrations.

Grandmother cannot guide me now, as we separated at the moment of retrieval, but she's waiting for me on the *other* side.

There are voices everywhere.

"Pick me. *Pick* me. Pick *me*."

"Not now," I grumble, and keep on wading through the mire.

What's the status?

A thin shadow cowers in my peripheral field of view, as another shade soars over it. Feathery creatures, snuffling snouts and wicked whispers ooze from the matrix. Some of these beings are incomplete, faded, lost. Others are desperate wholes. I stride onwards.

Is there a crossmatch?

Twenty retrievals ago, I thought I was master of all possible landscapes within the Compost Elevator. I believed the souls and spirits within were to be pitied. Seeking adventure, I looked to hone my art on brilliant deduction, intellectual virtuosity and with a clear sense of what was 'right' and 'timely'.

I exchanged this notion for a world of vibrations, confusion and chemical languages in which I am an avatar, not an expert.

Will's soul substance is strengthening, rippling against my own. I move even faster onwards. We're always running out of time.

"Pick me. *Pick* me. Pick *me*."

"Shhhh, I'm busy," I say to a cluster of needy ectoplasms.

Have all samples been accounted for?

A thousand dreams pass and fade around us: rooms with dead switches; hide-and-seek; a man's best friend; tangle of roots; a pitiless hurricane; glass insects; a nondescript cul-de-sac and an old tooth. Life, death, landscapes, cosmos.

I can't work with a blunt instrument. Someone change it.

In distant spaces, I feel people working, peering, stitching and the whirr of robotic arms. Lights are dancing around us, and through us.

A laser slices open the air. A lucky miss.

(Whispering).

"Come on, Will," I say, staggering through the oozing cavities.

Serous fluid puddles around us. Fibrin strands twist into long, ropey strands behind us, which cling to us, slowing us down.

"Pick me. *Pick* me. Pick *me*."

"Not now," I say, to a pitiful, partial soul that fades in despair.

I don't care who the insurer is. We're doing it my way. It's research.

Will's pulse is growing. We must synchronise our energy fields, otherwise our energies will dissipate, and he'll hold me back.

"Let's get it together," I say.

Time twists around us, as we're doused with solutions, hormones, tissue factors, stem cells – the interstices here are clogged, like sewers.

Can that person in the green scrub mask take a step back? You're in the light.

This is not a re-birthing.

Turn that machine down a few notches? It's burning my face off.

We're making our way back to the living realm through the cloning route and it's a highly convoluted journey.

Check the serial number on this with me, please.

It's hard to know what-organ-is-what.

Can whoever has the framework protocol please make sure everyone can see it. This must all be done at once.

"Are you still with me, Will?" I yell, but he does not respond and is even stronger than before. If I can't pull him through, then his life-force is going to drag me back and keep me here – indefinitely.

Just ahead, robotically-spun fragments of brain, heart, skin and bone becoming tissues and organs start to surround me.

This chemical suturing needs absolute concentration. Everyone keep quiet!

We're getting closer.

Debride that stuff, it's inviable.

Somewhere nearby bodies are entwined, sobbing, breaking news.

Check that culture is taking.

The space is firmer here. We're likely wrapped in soft plastic.

This is the delicate bit.

Body architects, surgeons, medics all make the switch from life support to patient with a deafening *swoosh.*

Plunging into the escalating vibrations, I harness their resonant frequency and break us through the membrane.

And… here we go.

Rachel Armstrong

Erasure

Leaving same way that we came, Grandmother and I must tidy ourselves away after the important work's done. After all, we are just another part of the high-tech apparatuses that bring fortunate humans back from the afterworlds.

Signing Off

This recording, which is the property of Maidstone Health Authority, may be used for insurance, medical, or legal purposes. No responsibility or liability whatsoever will be accepted for use of the material and information contained in this report beyond its intended useage. Any breach of these conditions will be entirely at the reader's risk.

Destination

"William. William. We think you can hear us. Raise your hand, or blink your eyes, if you do."

Will drifts in and out of consciousness as the intensive care support stabilises his newly animated flesh. Having stabilised his vital signs over the course of several months, the wrappings around his chemical sutures are removed and finally, he is transferred to an observation area in recovery.

"We thought to cut this ring from his hand, but it seems to have loosened," says a staff nurse to Peter, who is waiting patiently for his son to come around. "I suggest you put it somewhere safe."

Will's eyes flicker, but he doesn't open them.

"Son, can you hear me?"

Only the machinery appears to be breathing.

"It's your father, Will. I'm here right beside you. Whatever it is that you're going through, I want you to know I'm here with you."

Peter squeezes his hand.

"Will, you know I'm not sentimental and sometimes I've been tough on you."

A bead of moisture evaporates on his cheek.

"I'm begging you, come back to us, son, Joe, Natalie and me. We will be here to give you strength, just like you did for all of us when your mother passed."

Peter blots his nose on his sleeve.

"You made Natalie a cancer *survivor*, I'm not sure we ever told you, but it's true. Before you came into the world her outlook was so bleak that, while she was having her radiotherapy treatment, a priest came and read passages from the Bible over her. Just think of that. Natalie putting up with God's opinion."

Peter smiles, shakes his head.

"As your guardian, you brought out the fight in her. It wasn't easy, but she beat it in the end. It wasn't just Natalie, though, son. You gave Joe and me a reason to keep on going too, and I know meant the world to your mother."

Noticing the ring on the bedside locker, Peter presses his hands to his face.

"Your mother was a force of nature. She could do *anything* she set her mind to. Knowing her never quite felt *real*. For the short time I knew her, I felt responsible for her and somehow, understood she wouldn't be long in this world. Perhaps it was her love of the stars and wanting a life among them. When she left us, I kept a ring of hers for you. Perhaps foolishly, I thought if you wore it, she'd look after you. Oh, God, I'd do anything to bring you back."

Will's eyes flicker.

Peter studies Will's face as his head moves, first to the left, then slowly back to the right. His lips are twitching.

"Hey, nurse!" shouts Peter, over at the desk. "He's coming around."

Watching the flurry of activity at the desk, Peter raises his hand for attention.

Will opens his eyes, focusing on things around the room.

"Can I have some water?"

Peter holds the cup to Will's lips until he's certain that he can manage by himself.

The nursing staff check his vital signs and fluff the pillows around him.

"Do you need anything, sir?"

Peter shakes his head.

They enjoy each other's company in silence for a while.

"What do you remember about the crash, son?"

"Crash?" says Will.

"Your car was a total mess."

"I was going slowly."

"Your AI went berserk and flipped you head-on into a tree."

"I remember skidding," says Will. "And, yes, the crazy AI but only after I stopped. It couldn't have caused any harm."

"Well, whatever happened, for a while back then, you were a total mess. Officially dead. They called me for permission to enter you into a research programme using an advanced cloning technology. I didn't really understand what was involved but I consented. I'd already lost you."

Will is silent, then says, "I wasn't *really* dead, Dad. Was I?"

"Technically, yes. They cloned up parts of your flesh and brain, while they had you on life-support. You wouldn't be here without these advanced life procedures. Don't you recall anything at all? The surgeons said that sometimes people do."

"This is all so hard to make sense of," says Will, shaking his head.

He lifts his head and drops it back on the pillow, in a weak attempt to sit up.

"Not yet, son," says Peter. "You've a way to go yet."

"There's one thing, Dad," says Will, "you'll think I'm crazy."

"Go on."

"The doctors didn't save me. Someone else did."

"What do you mean, son?"

"When I think about it now, I can remember lights. I was sucked into an incredible void that stretched out forever. Two starlights spun around one another and filled the whole of reality. It was the saddest and most derelict place you could imagine. Even a single kind word, or touch in that place would have burst all your emotions."

Peter squeezes his hand.

"A terrible, suffocating nothingness was closing in on me and I knew, at any moment, it would swallow me up completely. Then, from nowhere, a woman stepped out in front of me, and stopped me."

"A woman?"

"I didn't recognise her, but it was someone I loved."

"Describe her," says Peter, "as best you can."

"She was wearing something white. When she stood blocking my path, I felt that I was being welcomed home."

"What else?"

"She left. No, *melted* before I could ask her where we were going. We were going somewhere together but I don't know where. The next thing I knew, it was all beeping, mumbling, tubes and technicians everywhere. That got my attention, for sure."

"I'm so glad you're back," says Peter, taking Will's hand in both of his own. "I won't lose you again."

Tolerance

It's been a long time since we
Considered ourselves human.
We're not ashamed, it's just that
Even in life, most of our cells are
Actually, symbionts and parasites.
Our chimeric origins reside in deep
Time, when one microbe swallowed
Another and couldn't digest it properly.
When we think of it, we are nearly
Walking restaurants, nourishing more
Creatures than we dare consider.
Our most numerous cells are
Microbes that live inside our gut,
Assimilating our food, making vitamins,
Regulating our mood and appetite.
Demodex spiders crawl on every
Square centimetre of our smooth
Skin and, while we sleep, they creep
Across our faces to nibble on dermal
Bugs, mate and lay eggs in our pores.
We don't even want to mention the
Three different types of lice that live
On our scalp, pubic hair and eyelashes.
Evolving together, this deep tolerance
Means 'we' are always part of 'others'.

Changes

Grandmother's taking forever to pass St. Andrew's House on Barming Heath. The harder the rain seems to fall, the more she lingers. Our lives beyond the hospital feels mostly spent under umbrellas.

He broke my jaw twice. I didn't say so, though. There was no help if I told anyone anyway. I said I'd fallen over.

"Come on," I say. "We'll only get the details of this new case when we arrive."

I learned to hide my feelings, because if I cried I was hit.

"Patience, child," She says. "We must always acknowledge the tormented voices of vagrant souls."

I wanted to punish myself, so I abused my own body. I lost count of the times I stuck a bread knife in myself and opened up my arms. I had no pain, no nothing.

"Of *course*," I say, "but I also can't wait to discover something new about the Compost Elevator."

As we pass through the entranceway, the hospital staff smirk a greeting at us and inwardly wonder whether we have souls, but things are different now than they were before.

They're coming!

Following my twenty-first retrieval, I expected to gain wisdom, or virtuosity.

Instead, I acquired voices.

Do anything you want to.

"We'll do it together."

These are not random inner monologues from passers-by, but my very own community of souls. Clinging to me weightlessly like an aura, they speak like my very own thoughts.

There is nobody better than you are.

"We enjoy good company."

Grandmother says they came back with me, because I attempted to retrieve more than one soul.

At first, they were mostly angry and afraid, while others were hopeless, but when we offered them a *home* with us, they started to flourish. Some of them will never become 'whole', but many others will one day re-enter the webs of life and death along the reincarnation pathway.

We love you.

"We love you, too."

They stay behind with Grandmother when I'm in retrieval mode, so I'm not weighed down. She doesn't mind looking after them for a while, even if it does require a certain amount of multi-tasking. Sometimes she is reluctant to hand them back, or perhaps they are loath to leave.

The older you are, the harder it is to let souls go.

Founding a sanctuary has never been our intention, but we welcome their company as a constant reminder that we are not one, but many beings.

The true *comedy* of our situation is that, despite all the contradictions, tribulations, and tragedy that lurk within the Compost Elevator's mischievous realm, life's epic transformations continue to give us all hope that *anything* can happen, and together, *everything* is still to play for.

About the Author

Rachel Armstrong is Professor of Experimental Architecture at the School of Architecture, Planning and Landscape, Newcastle University, United Kingdom, her day-to day work explores how our buildings can incorporate some of the properties of living systems to become 'living architectures'. She was also coordinator for the FET Open *Living Architecture* project (April 2016 – June 2019) and the EU Innovation Fund *ALICE*. Her fiction writing is an exploration of themes within her research, discovering what it means to inhabit different kinds of worlds – visible and invisible. She is a Rising Waters II Fellow with the Robert Rauschenberg Foundation (April-May 2016), Fellow of the British Interplanetary Society (2016), TWOTY futurist 2015, and a 2010 Senior TED Fellow. She is also a Member of the Hub for Biotechnology in the Built Environment at Newcastle University and Director and founder of the Experimental Architecture Group (EAG) whose work has been published and exhibited internationally. Previous titles in the 'Songs of the Ecocene' series include *Origamy* (2018) and *Invisible Ecologies* (2019).

NEW FROM NEWCON PRESS

Ian Whates – Dark Angels Rising

The Dark Angels – a notorious band of brigands turned folk heroes who disbanded a decade ago – are all that stands between humanity and disaster. Reunited, Leesa, Jen and their fellow Angels must prevent a resurrected Elder – last of a long dead alien race – from reclaiming the scientific marvels of his people. Supported by a renegade military unit and the criminal zealots Saflik, the Elder is set on establishing itself as God over all humankind.

Kim Lakin-Smith – Rise

Denounced by her own father and charged with crimes against the state, Kali Titian – pilot, soldier, and engineer – is sentenced to Erbärmlich prison camp, where she must survive among her fellow inmates the Vary, a race she has been raised to consider sub-human; a race facing genocide; a race who until recently she was routinely murdering to order. A potent tale of courage against the odds and the power of hope in the face of racial intolerance.

Liz Williams – Comet Weather

Practical Magic meets *The Witches of Eastwick*. A tale of four fey sisters set in contemporary London, rural Somerset, and beyond. The Fallow sisters: scattered like the four winds but now drawn back together, united in their desire to find their mother, Alys, who disappeared a year ago. They have help, of course, from the star spirits and the no-longer-living, but such advice tends to be cryptic and is hardly the most dependable of guides.

RB Kelly – Edge of Heaven

Creo Basse, a city built to house the world's dispossessed. In the dark, honeycomb districts of the lower city, Turrow searches for black-market meds for his epileptic sister when he encounters one of the many ways Creo can kill a person. A tinderbox of unrest finally ignites when a deadly plague breaks out, which the authorities claim is a terrorist weapon manufactured by extremist artificial humans hiding in the city, but is the truth darker still?

IMMANION PRESS
Purveyors of Speculative Fiction

Breathe, My Shadow by Storm Constantine

A standalone Wraeththu Mythos novel. Seladris believes he carries a curse making him a danger to any who know him. Now a new job brings him to Ferelithia, the town known as the Pearl of Almagabra. But Ferelithia conceals a dark past, which is leaking into the present. In the strange old house, Inglefey, Seladris tries to deal with hauntings of his own and his new environment, until fate leads him to the cottage on the shore where the shaman Meladriel works his magic. Has Seladris been drawn to Ferelithia to help Meladriel repel a malevolent present or is he simply part of the evil that now threatens the town? ISBN: 978-1-912815-06-7 £13.99, $17.99 pbk

The Lord of the Looking Glass by Fiona McGavin

The author has an extraordinary talent for taking genre tropes and turning them around into something completely new, playing deftly with topsy-turvy relationships between supernatural creatures and people of the real world. 'Post Garden Centre Blues' reveals an unusual relationship between taker and taken in a twist of the changeling myth. 'A Tale from the End of the World' takes the reader into her developing mythos of a post-apocalyptic world, which is bizarre, Gothic and steampunk all at once. Following in the tradition of exemplary short story writers like Tanith Lee and Liz Williams, Fiona has a vivid style of writing that brings intriguing new visions to fantasy, horror and science fiction. ISBN: 978-1-907737-99-2, £11.99, $17.50 pbk

The Heart of the Moon by Tanith Lee

Clirando, a celebrated warrior, believes herself to be cursed. Betrayed by people she trusted, she unleashes a vicious retaliation upon them and then lives in fear of fateful retribution for her act of cold-blooded vengeance. Set in a land resembling Ancient Greece, in this novella Tanith Lee explores the dark corners of the heart and soul within a vivid mythical adventure. The book also includes 'The Dry Season' another of her tales set in an imaginary ancient world of the Classical era.
ISBN: 978-1-912815-05-0 £10.99, $14.99 pbk

www.immanion-press.com
info@immanion-press.com

www.ingramcontent.com/pod-product-compliance
Lightning Source LLC
Chambersburg PA
CBHW030107260626
47156CB00008B/2567